A Doo Wop Mystery

STEVE LEADLEY

A Beach Reeds Publication

This book is a work of historical fiction.
Names, characters, places, and incidents
are either products of the author's imagination
or are used in a historical context to further the story's plot.
The actions and words of any and all actual personages herein are
to be construed as fictitious.

A Beach Reeds publication

Look for other books by Steve Leadley at:

www.steveleadleyauthorpage.weebly.com

ISBN: 978-0-9800944-9-7

Library of Congress Cataloging-in-Publication Data
Leadley, Steve
A Doo Wop Mystery/Steve Leadley
Beach Reeds, 2017

Historical Fiction/American Nostalgia/Doo Wop/ Historical Mystery

Cover photo courtesy of the Wildwood Historical Society

Acknowledgements

I must mention some of the wonderful people and excellent resources that were crucial in writing this story.

First, the books: Rob Ascough and Al Alvin's Images of America book: *Hunt's Pier.* Scott Hand and Diane Pooler's Images of America book: *Fun Pier 1957 to Adventure Pier.* Anita Hirsch's *Wildwood-By-The-Sea: Nostalgia and Recipes.* David Francis' *Wildwood by the Sea: The History of an American Resort* and Kirk Hastings' *Doo Wop Motel: Architectural Treasures of the Wildwoods.*

Local periodicals were also valuable resources, such as: *The Press of Atlantic City, Shore News Today, The Herald,* and *The Gazette* and Dorothy McMonagle Kulisek's exceptional *Wildwood Sun By the Sea.*

A number of wonderful websites were also instrumental in establishing authenticity: Ralph Grassi's *Funchase* website, Bill Cherkasky's *Dark in the Park* website, Wildwoodhistory.org by Maureen Cawley, *Wildwood Doo Wop.com.* Al Alven's *Wildwood 365blogspot.com, The Boardwalk Blog and Wildwoodvideoarchive.com.*

In addition to the aforementioned websites I must thank all those who have established Facebook pages dedicated to the Wildwoods and all of those who have posted videos online featuring their old home movies of vacations in the Wildwoods.

I also need to thank the staff of the George F. Boyer Museum and the Wildwood Historical Society, notably Pam

Bross, and Kathy Skouras, Larry Lillo and most especially the gracious help provided by Anne Vinci.

If there is anyone I left out or any resource I neglected to mention, I apologize.

<u>Dedication</u>

This book is affectionately dedicated to all who have had the pleasure of spending time in the Wildwoods. I hope that you enjoy the story itself but also that the setting and descriptions within evoke fond and nostalgic memories.

SL

Chapter I

<u>Anglesea, North Wildwood</u>

The sun had just begun to dip behind the tree-line that separated the mainland from the southernmost of New Jersey's barrier islands. As the amber disc descended, the marshes of the inland waterway assumed fantastic shades of burnt orange; the kind of color thought possible only in watercolor paintings.

There was a great deal of bustle in the lot. Couples and whole families slithered between the parked cars like mice through a maze. The slamming of car doors thudded a staccato beat. A boy in a coonskin hat narrowly avoided banging into one of the opening doors as he chased his sister, his cap pistol popping off rounds as he went. Even though it was late for dinner, the stream heading toward the restaurant was every bit as constant as the flow exiting the establishment.

A burly man in a dark suit and wide-brimmed gray fedora hiked up his sleeve and then grumbled a curse, noticing that he had forgotten his watch. A smile creased his lips however when he peered up at the large red and white neon sign at the corner of the lot that read: "Welcome to Zaberville." An oversized facsimile of a pocket watch was part of the signage. The clock face read 8:28. He was on time.

He stepped from the curb and joined the crowd crossing the street to the restaurant's entrance. Stopping short, he cast his first real glance at the building itself. It was huge;

1

but it didn't look like it always had been. The structure was an odd array of additions that gave the place a campy attraction. The front door was on a corner; another quirk for this odd landmark and as he approached it he passed by the skull of a Texas longhorn affixed to an outer wall. Waiting his turn to step inside, he looked up at the large reproduction of an eagle that sat atop the entranceway, its wings swept backwards as if it were about to swoop down and satisfy its own voracious appetite by carrying off one of the children on the step.

"Welcome to Zaberer's," the hostess announced with a congenial smile.

"I'm supposed to meet somebody," he returned in a gravelly voice. "Oh, I see him. Thanks anyway," he said, briskly brushing by the woman and making off toward a nearby table where a man with a red and black striped tie sat under the colored glass of a Tiffany light.

"I'm lucky you was sitting up front. I never would've seen you otherwise," he said, depositing himself in one of the chairs at the red and white checked tablecloth. He pulled his hat from his head, dropping it on a corner of the table. "How big is this place?" he wondered aloud.

"Oh, there are a dozen or so dining rooms. They serve a few thousand people each night."

"It's weird. I'll say that for it." His head swiveled around, taking in a child sitting atop a statue of a green and white lion before peering up at a perch holding a three foot high cartoon mouse figurine dressed in Mexican attire.

The man with the striped tie chuckled as he passed a menu across the table. "You get more than good food for your money. You get atmosphere; you get Zaberized," he smiled.

"You get what?"

2

"Zaberized. Ed Zaberer. *The Host of the Coast*," he said, pointing at the picture on the menu.

"Hey! Hey! Isn't that Jimmy Durante who just walked in?" the newcomer asked enthusiastically as his gruff negativity seemed to evaporate at the sight of the celebrity.

"Sure, and back there," his tablemate pointed over his shoulder to a corner where a handsome dark-haired man was seated amongst a group. "Is the host of General Electric Theater."

"Ronald Reagan?" the other man asked, standing briefly to confirm the fact.

"How about a drink before you order?"

"Yeah," he turned to the waitress who had just arrived. "Let me have a seven and seven."

After the server left, the newcomer's serious, brusque demeanor returned. "So," he said, lighting up a cigarette. "Let's get down to business."

The other man leaned forward surreptitiously, a solemn expression clouding his features. In a subdued tone he said, "I've been told you're the man for the job." He peered intently across the table. "I want him gone-- to disappear without a trace."

The bustle and noise created the environment of excited confusion he always felt in rail stations. As a kid, he'd been entranced by trains. Heck, what boy hadn't? Sure, he wasn't a child anymore, but the wonder and exhilaration had stayed with him. He marveled at the hundreds of people scurrying to and fro, bound for points unknown. They had either just ridden, or were about to board, the great steel beasts whose pathways spread out across the landscape like a giant web. The stitch-work of ties and rails had linked once distant regions and divergent states into a cohesive nation. Even having seen the great rail depots of Germany couldn't dampen his enthusiasm for his first time at 30th Street Station.

"Hey, watch it, bub," a man grumbled when he stopped short upon stepping into the main concourse. Ignoring the comment, his eyes widened at the sheer expanse of the nearly three-hundred foot long room. His head tilted back and he stood admiring the coffered ceiling. The art deco lamps that hung from the waffle pattern added a 1920s flair that distinguished the fixtures from the giant, severe, five story windows that rimmed the hall.

"Come on, fella," a man wearing a homburg hat urged as he brushed past the impressed visitor.

He smiled bashfully to himself, realizing that his inner-child needed to be restrained. With a slight chuckle, he hefted his bag and headed down the great hall. As he neared the end however, his progress slowed once more as he reached the huge forty foot high winged bronze statue of the Archangel Michael lifting a fallen soldier. Suddenly a cloud that had been loitering over the sun continued on its way, and bright beams of sunlight pierced the high row of windows along the western wall. The streaming shafts bathed the monument, giving the visage of God's envoy a dreamlike realism.

"Hey! Hey, Rick!"

The spellbound young man shook off his wonder and turned to see a dark-haired fellow advancing in his direction.

"Rick! What 'cha doin'? Waiting for it to take off?" the new arrival smiled, as he roughly patted his friend's

4

shoulder with his left hand while pumping his right in a welcoming shake.

"Just admiring the heavenly wonders of Philadelphia," Rick returned, a warm grin expanding across his face.

"Ma, che sei grullo?," the dark-haired boy blurted in Italian. "How crazy are you? You want a heavenly wonder in Philly?" he smirked. "Wait 'til you get a bite of a cheesesteak."

"Alright, Vinny," Rick replied. "I heard you talk enough about Philly food to get my mouth watering more than once. Now it's time to put up. I'm starving. How about one of those cheesesteaks right now?"

Vinny pulled the suitcase from his friend's hand and began leading him toward the huge row of glass doors that fronted the station. "Na, not now. You're in for an even better treat. My ma is cooking dinner. Those Italian joints we ate at in West Germany? They got nothin' on my ma. Come on," he motioned toward the exit.

The pair of army buddies navigated the throng of travelers and stepped out onto Market Street. Rick's eyes climbed the giant stone columns that ascended to support the station's portico. "This place makes the Brandenburg Gate look shoddy," he thought to himself as he walked on, nearly tripping down the steps.

"Come on; agitate the gravel, will you?" Vinny's voice had a pleading tone to it. "My stomach's growlin' like a bearcat engine."

"Hey, nice rod!" Rick admired as the sunlight dazzled off of the chrome of a red and white convertible Bel Air. "Is this yours?" he asked as his friend deposited his satchel in the rear seat. The car was about five years old, but that didn't take away from its beauty.

Vinny laughed. "I wish! My uncle's been out of town for a few weeks so he loaned it to me."

The pair climbed into the coupe and Vinny inserted the key. The warm rumble of the 265 cubic inch V8 found accompaniment as the radio glowed to life. "This is Hy Lit coming to you from Wibbage, WIBG Philadelphia, ready to take you back to the Stone Age with the Hollywood Argyles. Here's *Alley Oop*." The familiar backing vocals that begin the popular tune echoed from the car's speakers as the Bel Air smoothly swung away from the curb, its automatic "power glide" transmission shifting into second as they advanced into traffic.

Vinny had taken the Schuykill Expressway to pick his friend up in Center City, but on the way he noticed a four car pileup on the southbound side, so returning the same way was out of the question. The afternoon sun glinted off of the chrome "hood bird" as the ornament pointed the way up Market Street.

"Hey, what's that? City Hall?" Rick asked as the Chevy swung into the loop that circled the huge, ornate building.

"Sure is," the native replied, passing the massive John Wannamaker store and turning onto South Broad Street. "Wait another couple of seconds and we'll be far enough away that you can see William Penn."

"William Penn?"

"His statue. Cast an eyeball atop City Hall."

Before a minute had expired Rick's craning neck allowed him to focus in on the icon of the Quaker patriarch peering out over his "City of Brotherly Love."

First Ricky Nelson and then the Fleetwoods wafted from the convertible as it made its way toward South Philadelphia. "Hey, Hy Lit comin' at ya again from my perch at Wibbage. You can expect a high approaching the mid-eighties tomorrow with bright sunny skies. Tonight is going to be a muggy one, though. Let's hope you don't have what ails Jimmy Clanton! Here he is with *Another Sleepless Night*."

It wasn't long before the red and white Chevy was hanging a left onto Oregon Avenue. "Hey, nice park," Rick observed, peering toward his right.

"Yeah, that's Marconi Plaza. Marconi is like second to Columbus as a hero to the Italians of South Philly."

"What about the Pope?" Rick asked with a wink.

Vinny's lips creased to expose his pearly whites. "Oh, well the Pope is certainly number one. But John the 23rd is an Italian. Not for nothing, but should a non-Italian gain the papacy again one day... the Pope may slip a few notches-- at least in my neighborhood."

The South Philadelphian made a right onto Darien Street. The block was alive with activity. Three young girls were engaged in some artistic chalk-work on the sidewalk as a lad in a cowboy hat leisurely circled them on his tricycle. In less than thirty feet the Bel Air came up behind a manhole cover that was serving as home plate in a stickball game. "Hey Carmen," Vinny yelled affectionately as he propped himself up, his diminutive frame cresting the chrome rim of the windshield. "Move it for a minute, I'm comin' through!"

"Yo, Vin!" The lanky fourteen-year-old greeted. "Don't ya want to wait and see this?" he called back to the car. I'm gonna take Frankie deep again."

"Yeah, yeah, keep talkin,'" the pitcher returned, bouncing the ball in front of him.

"I can smell my ma's cutlets from here," Vinny replied. "You make me late for dinner and I'm telling her it was your fault."

7

That was all it took for the batter to abandon his spot. With a look of feigned fear, Carmen hustled to the sidewalk and the fielders up the street followed suit. Vinny passed a few open spots. "That kid can hit, I'm not running the risk of a dent in my uncle's car." He turned the corner onto Johnston Street before parking. "Help me with the top, will you?" he said as he snapped off the ignition.

Within a minute the pair were walking back down Darien Street, Rick's light brown hair towering a good eight inches above the dark, shiny mop of his friend. The boy in deep "center field" bent to tie the dangling lace of his Ked when Carmen connected with a blast. The fielder suddenly stood and took a step but tripped over his errant shoestring.

"Get it!" Vinny urgently commanded, slapping Rick's bicep with the back of his hand.

"Huh?" the stranger confusedly replied.

Vinny tried to push by his tall companion but banged into him, sending both to the ground. The ball landed on the sidewalk on the far side of the street before bouncing into a corner where the five steps of a stoop ascended to adjoin to its row house. A skinny old man who looked to be in his eighties had been sitting on the stoop and with the vigor of someone a quarter of his age, scurried from the step and grabbed the ball with his left hand. In his right appeared a knife. With the dexterity of a professional apple peeler, he made quick work of the orb, leaving a tangled ribbon as its only remnant. The old fellow let fly with a string of loud exclamations in Italian, brandishing the knife over his head as a victorious gladiator might have done with his sword.

"Aw Vin, why didn't you get it?" whined the boy who's uncooperative sneaker had caused the unfortunate demise of their plaything.

"I tried, Anthony. Sorry." He shrugged his shoulders and patted the boy on the back.

A cacophony of derisive jibes echoed down the street from the mouths of the players. Some hurled invectives at the old man, others at Anthony for not getting the ball in time. Their cracks were cut short however as several doors opened at nearly at the same time, as if on cue, calling the kids in for supper.

"What the heck was that all about?" Rick asked. He cast a perplexed expression in the direction of the old man, who stood atop his stoop nodding with his arms folded across his chest like Mussolini from the balcony.

"Aaah," Vinny waved a dismissive hand in the codger's direction. "That's Joe the Ballcutter." He said it as if it were an official title. "He's a jerk. Can't stand the guys playing on the street. He wants them to go over to the schoolyard. So anytime a ball touches his house, he makes with the knife."

Rick shook his head at what he considered a surreal situation. He opened his mouth to speak but was interrupted by his friend.

"Hey, I really did catch a whiff of my ma's cutlets. I bet if the wind was right I could've smelled them from Broad Street. Come on," he urged, giving his pal a friendly shove. He broke into a jog and Rick quickly followed as he bounded up the steps of a row house in the middle of the block.

As Rick walked in through the foyer he was met with the aroma his friend had allegedly picked up much earlier. And since his stomach reacted with a rumble, he suspected

Vinny's comments about his mother's cooking abilities were more than idle boasting. When Rick exited the foyer into the living room he nearly collided into the back of a short, balding man wearing a white, ribbed tank undershirt. The man was busy banging the ceiling with the handle end of a broom. It didn't take much deductive skill to realize his actions were in response to the overly loud sound of Bobby Rydell's *Swingin' School* reverberating down to the parlor. Turning, the patriarch expressed his exasperation to the newcomers. "Basta!" he said, as much with his hands as with his mouth. "Vincent! Your sister; with that music!"

"Hey Pop," the younger, thinner, version of the man said, ignoring his father's outburst, "This is the friend I was telling you about; Rick Walker."

"Hello, Mr. Valenti."

"Oh. Good to meet you." Vinny's father transferred the broom to his left hand and shook the one extended by his son's companion.

"Georgie," Vinny called to the nine-year-old boy reclining on the plastic covered sofa. "This is my buddy, Rick." The boy dipped his comic book enough to nod at the guest.

Just then a thin, dark-haired woman in a housecoat and apron burst into the room. "Angelina!" she yelled. "Giorgio," she said, turning to the boy. "Go get your sister. Tell her to set the table." The youngster put aside his comic and scurried upstairs.

"Hey, Ma. This is my friend, Rick."

An expression of surprise sprung to the woman's face as she had been oblivious that her eldest son had returned home. She came over and gave his ear an affectionate tug. "How are you?" she asked as she turned toward Rick. Before he could answer, she followed with, "Hungry, I hope." As suddenly as she had emerged, she disappeared again back into the kitchen.

A moment later the music emanating from the second floor abruptly ceased. Vinny's father clasped his hands in praise and then sank into an easy chair, returning to his half read newspaper. The youngest Valenti fairly flew down the stairs and vaulted back onto the sofa, returning to his illustrated adventure tale. Finally, a pretty ponytailed fourteen-year-old came bouncing down the steps. She almost froze when she spied the handsome young man with her brother but quickly recovered her poise as she reached the landing before the final two steps.

"Angel, this is my friend, Rick. You know, the guy you drooled over in the photo of me and him in West Berlin," he winked at his buddy.

The girl turned beat red. "Vincent!" she gasped, before storming through the swinging door that led to the kitchen at the rear of the house.

"I've got myself set up in the basement," Vinny said. "This one took over the room when I was overseas," he continued, jerking a thumb in the direction of his brother. "Come on, let's put your bag down there and get the cot set up."

The pair had barely accomplished their tasks when a call echoed through the house that dinner was ready. Vinny and Rick made the climb back up to the main floor and seated themselves at the kitchen table along with Vinny's dad and brother. The Valenti women were still at work. Mrs. Valenti was placing two bowls of marinated olives on the table and Angelina circled the group with a pitcher, filling their glasses.

"So, you served with Vincent in the Army, eh?" the senior Valenti asked, popping an olive into his mouth.

"Yes, sir," Rick replied as Vince offered the bowl of olives in his direction.

"Shoot anybody?" Georgie chimed in, his eyes brightening at the possibility.

Rick never answered the question as a small plate of spaghetti, smothered in red sauce appeared in front of him. All members of the family were now seated and he followed Vinny's example of swirling the strands around his fork before depositing the pasta into his waiting mouth.

"You're from Illinois, then?" Mr. Valenti asked between bites.

"Um, no. Ohio."

"Come to see the Jersey shore, eh?" the patriarch asked.

"Oh, I wish I was going with you!" Angel pouted.

"Angelina!" her mother interjected. "You *are* going. You know we go every August."

"Oh, I know, I just wish I was going *now*."

"Vinny, er ah, Vincent, told me an awful lot about Wildwood when we were stationed in West Germany. It sounds like a great place."

"Oh, it is! Wait until you see!" Angelina confirmed.

Rick had barely cleaned his plate of the delicious pasta when Vinny's mother replaced it with one containing a veal cutlet and a side of vegetables.

"Hey, Vin," Georgie said, pointing a fork at his brother. "Phone back and let me know if there's any new rides on the amusement piers."

"I will," Vincent replied. "Maybe if there are, you can ride The Flyer a few less times this year."

"Yeah, that'll be the day," Angelina added, rolling her eyes.

"What's The Flyer?" asked Rick.

12

"It's a roller coaster on Hunt's Pier; and this one," Vinny nodded toward his brother, "must've ridden it fifteen times when we were there last summer."

"Twelve," the youngest Valenti corrected with pride. "Rick, it's a boss ride. If you like roller coasters, you've got to check it out."

"I'll make sure that I do," he smiled, admiring the youth's enthusiasm.

After dinner the two friends unfolded a pair of aluminum lawn chairs on the sidewalk outside of the Valenti home. Rick eased into the crisscrossed webbing and patted his stomach. "Well, I've got to give it to you. Your mom is some kind of cook. That sauce..." he licked his lips at the memory. "Mmm."

"Sauce," Vinny quipped. "What a metagon! Gravy, brother; Italians call it gravy."

"Well call it what you will, it was great."

The shadows from the line of row homes on the opposite side of the street were encroaching on the neighborhood but there was still enough light for the stickball game to reconvene after the dinner break.

"I guess they got another ball," Rick said, as a batter swung and missed.

"Yeah, when they run low they climb up on the roof and collect the ones that ended up there. Here," Vinny returned, handing his friend a can.

"Wishniak? What the heck is wishniak?" Rick asked, reading the label: *Frank's Black Cherry Wishniak Soda.*

"I have no idea," Vinny said, tugging loose the ring atop his own can. "But you're gonna like it."

A hiss breathed from the top of the can as Rick pealed back the aluminum ring. He took a swig. His face assumed a satisfied expression and he nodded approvingly before bringing the can back up to his lips for an encore. "Right again, Vin. I do like it." He tilted forward a bit and peered around a car to witness a neat catch by one of the fielders in the stickball game. "So," he said, leaning back again. "We're staying at your aunt's place in Wildwood?"

Vinny took a swallow of his own soda. "Not exactly. Aunt Marie is actually *my mom's* aunt. She's got a place in Wildwood; a rooming house and two detached efficiency units. We'll do some repair work for her and she'll let us stay no charge. We can work mornings and then have the rest of the day and the nights to ourselves."

"I see it now. Your dad let you off from the dry cleaner shop because you're doing a good deed for your mom's aunt."

"Kind of. The summer is slower at the shop. He doesn't need me as much. But there's more to it. When Aunt Marie asked for my help, he wasn't about to say no. My dad likes Wildwood as much as the rest of us but he's also a cheapskate. She allows our family to stay at off-season rates even in August and my pop isn't about to rile her and risk that deal."

"Well you've got me cranked up, that's for sure. I can't wait to get some sun and surf."

"The beaches are great," Vinny downed another gulp of soda. "But once the sun sets, there's still a lot of fun to be had. Not only is there the boardwalk, but the dancing and entertainment is top notch. They don't call Wildwood *Little Las Vegas* for nothing."

14

Photos courtesy of the Wildwood Historical Society

15

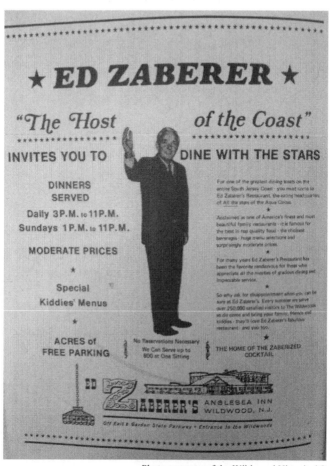

Photo courtesy of the Wildwood Historical Society

Chapter 2

"Okay, the luggage is in the trunk," Vinny reported, unlocking the door for his friend. He danced past the chrome bird on the hood of the Bel Air and opened the driver's side for himself.

Rick groaned a terrific yawn as he helped roll back the convertible top. "Aren't we going to eat?" he asked, lamenting their leaving the house without breakfast.

"We'll grab something, don't worry. If we'd eaten at the house, my ma would've kept feeding us for an hour. We had to cop a breeze and clear out of there if we want to get this rod on the road."

In a matter of minutes the Chevy had made two rights and was heading down Oregon Avenue. At a stop-light Vinny waved over a boy who had been standing in the island. The lad snatched a brown paper bag from the cardboard crate at his feet and the driver traded some silver for the bag. The exchange occurred with such commonplace efficiency, by the time the light glowed green the Bel Air was again in motion.

"Here," said Vinny, handing the bag to his buddy.

"What's this?"

"Breakfast."

Rick reached inside to find a row of tanned figure eights. "Hmm," he said, tugging one loose and handing it to Vinny before producing one for himself. "So this is a Philadelphia soft pretzel, huh?" He took a bite. "Hey, this is good."

"You don't have soft pretzels out in the heartland?" Vincent jibed.

17

"We have pretzels aplenty, but they're not soft. I like these better, to tell you the truth," he said, downing another swallow.

"I'm sure there are some mustard packets in the bottom of the bag, if that's the way you like 'em."

"I'm good. How about you?"

"Too messy while I'm driving. I'll stick with it plain."

The Walt Whitman Bridge loomed before them and as the car moved eastward across the span the bright morning sun dazzled off of the wide expanse of the Delaware River. Both friends, as if on cue, pulled sunglasses from a breast pocket and slid them on.

They munched their pretzels, sharing a thermos of coffee Vinny had astutely brought along. The news of the day blared from their radio as the handsome Chevy entered New Jersey and headed southeasterly down the Black Horse Pike.

"Oh man, not again," Vinny grumbled when the announcer informed that the Milwaukee Braves had beaten his beloved Phillies 3-2. The Phillies were going to be bad this year. Vinny knew that. Robin Roberts was all that remained of "The Whiz Kids" he had idolized as a child. Sure, he had matured into an adult but no man truly leaves his boyhood behind when it comes to baseball. He had not yet overcome the dejection he felt when over the winter the team had dealt his favorite player, Richie Ashburn, to the Cubs. There were some bright spots. The Phils had acquired Tony Tayor and Tony Gonzales and they still had Johnny Callison and Chris Short. But the projections were that the Phillies would finish last in the National League; a wound that could only be diminished by a strong showing by the Eagles during the upcoming football season. And fortunately, the Eagles had a real chance at the championship.

Rick wanted to needle his friend about the Phillies' loss but held back as the box scores continued to drift from the car speakers. When the announcer informed that his favorite team, the Cincinnati Reds, had been beaten too and by a much greater margin, his delay proved wise. The Reds weren't as bad as the Phillies this year, but they weren't that much better.

The ride through Southern New Jersey was a pleasant one. Rick inhaled a deep breath as he tilted his head back to take in the brilliant blue sky overhead. A dozen or so cotton ball-like puffs drifted lazily through the atmosphere like a grazing herd of heavenly sheep.

Vinny's favorite radio station, WIBG, kept them company with a never-ending supply of good music. The Everly Brothers were just finishing up *Cathy's Clown* when Vinny veered off, seeming to succumb to a series of signs that had appeared beside the roadway. The placards were hand-painted, each announcing a different bounty of the local farming community. Delicious Blueberries... Juicy Peaches... Sweet Corn... The descriptions alone were enough to kick Rick's salivary glands into action.

"Gotta stop for a minute. My aunt wouldn't forgive me if I didn't pick up some Jersey tomatoes on the way down," Vinny stated, pulling the car from the highway. The tires hissed in the sandy soil that fronted the roadside stand. "If we're lucky she'll use some to make a baked ziti," he smiled. "Her cooking rivals my ma's."

While Vinny made his way over to the angled bins that displayed the farm stand's wares, Rick exited his side of the car to stretch his legs. He had not taken two paces when a dark blue Desoto abruptly came to a stop in the spot next to him. The sedan's sudden appearance caused Rick to jump back a step.

"Oh, I'm sorry," the man apologized from his open window. "I almost ran you down!"

The woman sitting beside her husband turned to reprimand a boy of about nine seated on the rear bench seat. "You see what almost happened because of you? Your father told you to take it easy with that ball." The youngster wore a faded Phillies cap and was pounding a ball into a mitt.

"He's been pretending to make diving catches for the last two miles," the man said to Rick. "I'm about ready to strangle him."

"I'm okay. No harm done," Rick chuckled.

"Yeah, not yet," the father returned, leering at his son.

As Rick skirted the front of the sedan he heard the woman speak to her husband, "Fred, leave the car running. I like this song," she said, turning the radio up a notch. "Just get half a dozen apples."

Rick began strolling toward the end of the stand, half-heartedly examining the fruit and vegetables being offered.

The apples were some distance from their car and the woman's voice echoed loudly, "No, no. Not those. The other ones!" Rick turned to see her pointing and gesticulating from the passenger seat. "Don't you know anything?" she blurted before throwing her hands up in exasperation. With a huff that sounded like a locomotive releasing its steam, she opened her door and stomped off toward her struggling mate.

Rick shrugged and smiled at the example of one of those displays that makes some men cringe at the mention of the word "marriage."

As soon as the woman was away from the car the boy returned to his make-believe pantomime of saving the game with his acrobatic heroics. Unfortunately however, as he flopped across the cushy bench seat the ball got away from him. It careened off of the door panel and banged the gearshift, throwing the car from "park" into "reverse."

Suddenly the Desoto propelled backward. The woman turned from her apple inspection and let loose with a high-pitched shriek as the family auto rolled rearward toward the busy highway.

Without thinking, Rick took off toward the sedan. The boy in the backseat had begun to scream bloody murder, his eyes glued out the rear window where the view of the cars zooming back and forth along the Black Horse Pike foretold that doom awaited in mere moments.

Attempting to grab the door handle would mean the possibility of fumbling with it and losing the split seconds Rick did not have to spare. Therefore the young man did not slacken his pace as he made it to the car but rather dove head first through the passenger-side window, threading the needle with more luck than precision. Rick's right shoulder slammed into the bottom of the steering wheel and his momentum caused him to bounce off of the seat-back and tumble onto the floor.

Rick landed with his nose pinned to the floor mat. In desperation he struggled in the cramped space to twist himself to face the front of the auto. It was only a fraction of a moment before he accomplished his goal but it seemed to take an eternity. With all of his might, he thrust his right hand against the brake pedal. A squeal echoed through the floorboards as the car came to a stop inches from the busy highway.

"Hey!" Rick called to the screeching boy in the back seat. "Hey! Put the car in park!" the pinioned hero ordered, wondering if he could keep sufficient pressure on the brake in his awkward, confined position. Unfortunately the kid continued his wailing unabated. Suddenly the driver's side door opened and Rick caught a glimpse of a familiar pair of khaki slacks. The sound of the column shifter being moved quickly followed.

"I got it. It's in park."

"Whew," Rick spat forth, releasing the pedal. He dragged the back of his hand across his perspiration soaked forehead before rolling over to peer up at Vinny's concerned face.

After gracious thanks and an accepted offer to pay for Vincent's bag of tomatoes, the friends were back on the road again. As the sporty convertible cruised happily along, the driver tossed a small package to his pal.

"What's this?"

"A reward," Vinny smirked.

"Tandy Kake?"

"Just try it."

"Gee," Rick said with a feigned sheepishness in his voice. "You shouldn't have oughta done it. We got free tomatoes didn't we? I don't need a reward from you for saving that kid," he smiled.

"For saving the kid? Is that what you think? Na, it's for your Johnny Weissmuller impersonation. That dive you made through the window? Saturday night on the Late, Late Show I watched him make that same exact move rescuing Jane from some alligators."

"Crocodiles."

"What?"

"No alligators in Africa. They must've been crocodiles."

"What do they have on the back lot in Hollywood? Because that's where the Tarzan films were shot."

"Good point."

Rick removed the wrapper and bit the pastry in half. The combination of sponge cake, peanut butter and chocolate was a new sensation for him, but one he found delicious. "Another Philadelphia delicacy?" he asked as the rest of the first treat vanished beyond his lips.

"Tastykakes. You can't beat 'em," Vinny said, licking his lips.

It was not long before the Bel Air was leaving the Black Horse Pike and merging onto the Garden State Parkway. The Parkway had been completed some six years prior and the passionate planning of engineers and landscape architects had not been in vain. A wide median of placid slopes, teeming with foliage and flowers separated the two southbound lanes from their sisters headed in the other direction. The road provided a state of the art highway where motorists could safely travel at elevated speeds but the attention to maintaining a scenic route gave travelers the feel of a country road through the woodlands and wetlands of coastal New Jersey.

After some thirty miles the car moved off of the Parkway, making its final approach toward their destination. They joined the procession of autos traversing the thin causeway that spanned the distance between mainland New Jersey and the barrier island.

Rick peered out across the broad marshland. River-like ribbons shimmered as they cut serpentine paths through the great expanse of aquatic meadow. The car passed a family eating a picnic lunch by the side of the road, taking a break from their crabbing adventure. He caught the meaning, if not the words of the father's raised voice as he tried to get the children to the blanket instead of admiring their catch in a nearby peach basket.

The Chevy whisked by the crabbers and Rick sat up in his seat and raised his sunglasses for a better view of a snow-white bird stepping gingerly with its stilt-like legs through the high grass.

The young man inhaled deeply. The refreshing aroma of salt air filled him with contentment. That smell. He had never experienced the scent of the Jersey shore and it left an indelible mark on his senses. Years, even decades later, even a hint of that beach fragrance would bring an immediate smile to his lips.

The chrome bird on the Bel Air's hood inclined as they ascended the George Redding Bridge, the final obstacle separating vacationers from the island that held the Wildwoods. As they crested the structure, WIBG treated them to Elvis's rollicking *Stuck On You*.

From the bridge he spied a curious structure off to his right. He eyed the white building that fronted the inland waterway. The giant red letters indicated that it was a seafood restaurant called "Urie's Fish Fry." He turned to look back at the place as the Bel Air's tires touched the island, intrigued that the eatery stood on a foundation of pilings much like the amusement piers he hoped to visit.

Rick tried to play it cool as the convertible cruised down Rio Grande Avenue but his eyes were surreptitiously in motion behind his sunglasses, taking in the sights and sounds of the busy entranceway to the island. He was particularly interested in a futuristic looking L-shaped building to his left. A large neon sign read *Fantasy Motel*. The name was backlit with heavenly objects such as a planet, star and moon. This attention grabbing marquee sat upon a uniquely pitched roof that topped a lounge/game room. The lounge featured tall, panoramic windows that bordered a large second floor sun-deck offering a view of the sparkling swimming pool below.

Although he did not voice it, he was disappointed when the Chevy made a left onto Atlantic Avenue. He had hoped their path would take them all the way to the beach block so that he could catch sight of the ocean. He did get a glimpse of the famous boardwalk however, as Vinny drove a few blocks before making a left onto Burk Avenue. Midway up the block his friend swung the Bel Air into a concrete driveway that straddled a tan rooming house and two flat-topped efficiency units of the same color.

A hand-painted sign hung from an iron pole that extended from the larger building out over the sidewalk. The placard read: *Holly Beach House*. At the corners of the sign the artist had included green sprigs of the tree and its characteristic red berries.

"Here we are!" Vinny announced, smiling with satisfaction.

"Nice place," Rick observed. The rooming house on the left side of the driveway had a broad two story porch. A set of wooden stairs that paralleled the sidewalk ran up to the second level. The siding was of diamond-shaped shingles, painted an attractive sandy shade. However some of the wall was faded to a lighter color, revealing the angle at which the sun fell on the structure.

The efficiency units on the other side of the driveway were of the same tone as the rooming house but a more modern layer of stucco covered the surface. These apartments were connected as one building, running beside the length of the driveway; their front doors opening toward the concrete drive. A small grass plot sat between the street side wall of the first unit and the sidewalk. A small hedge, in need of some sculpting ran around the area, encircling a faded birdbath in the center of the yard.

"Ah, Vincenzo!" echoed as a screen door near the rear side of the rooming house banged open. A portly woman with silver hair and black rimmed eyeglasses hurried out, smiling infectiously.

"Hi, Aunt Marie," Vinnie called, stepping from the car.

The woman moved with the energy of a far younger person as she scurried up to her great-nephew and grabbed him in a bear hug. "This is my friend Rick; the one I was telling you about."

"Ah, from the army, yes? You look thin Vincenzo," she said, stepping back and mulling him over. "Come inside. I have some veal parmesan sandwiches." The mere mention of the food made Rick's stomach rumble in anticipation.

"So, Tony let you use his car, eh?" Aunt Marie said, stopping to look at the Bel Air. "I always knew you were his favorite nephew." She gave his cheek an affectionate pinch.

Vinny laughed. "I told him I needed it to come down and do some work on your place. I think it was more his fondness for *you* that got me use of the car! Hey, hold on," he reached for the brown bag in the back seat. "We've brought you some Jersey tomatoes."

"Oh, you're a good boy," his great-aunt said, giving his cheek another pinch.

After lunch the young men unpacked their gear into the first floor bedroom they were to share. After they had settled in, they surveyed the rest of property. There was some painting that needed to be done. The faded side of the house was the most apparent but both levels of the front porch had flaking paint on the spindles that lined the railing.

The rear of the house featured another staircase under which resided two outdoor showers. The doors were reluctant to open, and the friends agreed that new hinges would fix the problem. Behind the house there was a plot of grass spanned by three clotheslines. One of the metal poles was badly rusted and in danger of folding over if anything heavy was to be placed on that particular line. Apparently others had come to the same conclusion as only a light sheet occupied the space while clothing and thicker blankets and towels adorned the other lines.

"Hey Aunt Marie," Vinny called, moving over to the kitchen door.

"Yes?" the woman's silver hair materialized as she approached the screen.

"How many people do you have here now?"

"There are four upstairs. A couple is renting Unit 1," she pointed toward the efficiency unit closest to the street, "and a family of three is in Unit 2."

"You don't think we'll disturb anybody by working in the mornings do you?"

"Those in the efficiencies are here on vacation. They're up early and usually at the beach by ten or eleven. The kids in the house are here working. One is a mate on a fishing boat. He's gone early. The other three have jobs on the boardwalk. They work mostly nights but are usually on the beach pretty early. Upstairs has a kitchen and a bathroom that they all share. You'll probably only see them coming and going."

The friends found time that afternoon to clean out the shed at the back of the property and get the tools and workbench in order for their future jobs around the Holly Beach House. After a welcome shower and plentiful dinner the pair positioned themselves in a couple of the rockers on the front porch.

"Hey!" Vinny called out from behind the newspaper in his hands. "We've got to hit the Starlight tonight!"

"The Starlight?"

"Sure! The Starlight Ballroom. You're never going to guess who'll be there."

Rick scratched his head in mock contemplation. "I've ruled out President Eisenhower. I give up."

"Dick Clark!"

"Dick Clark! Really?"

"Yep. He's going to take up his old post tonight and spin the records at the hop."

"His old post..." Rick repeated. "Oh yeah, didn't he start American Bandstand in Wildwood?"

"Well in Philly really, but three years ago he brought his show to the Starlight Ballroom for the summer and the first national broadcast of Bandstand aired from the Starlight. He took off like a rocket after that of course. But tonight we're in for his nostalgic return."

Rick played with the small dial of the radio that sat on the nightstand between the two beds.

"Right there, leave that on," Vinny ordered when he heard *A Teenager in Love* by Dion and the Belmonts.

"Ok, but how long are you going to stand in front of that mirror? It doesn't matter how many times you run that comb through your hair; you're not going to get any better looking."

"You've got it backwards. I'm trying to style my mop so as to make myself look a little more ordinary. I want to give you at least a fighting chance with the ladies."

"Gee, thanks," Rick smiled. "Hey hand me that Old Spice, will you?"

Vinny grabbed the white bottle from the dresser and previewed some of his moves as he danced his way over to the bed where his friend sat. "Here you go, Daddy-O."

As Rick took his turn at the mirror *Trouble in Paradise* by The Crests came over the radio; an unknowing prelude to the mystery that was about to engulf the young men.

The Fantasy Motel

Photo courtesy of Anne Vinci

Photos courtesy of Anne Vinci

Chapter 3

As soon as Rick stepped onto the sidewalk in front of the Holly Beach House he could see the warm glow of the boardwalk radiating above the neighboring buildings. He smiled with anticipation as he and Vinny began walking up the street. They crossed Atlantic Avenue stopping for a minute to admire Memory Lane along the Atlantic Avenue side of Fox Park. Being veterans themselves, they were compelled to pause a moment to honor those who had lost their lives fighting for our country. After this brief interlude, they continued along Burk Avenue.

One more intersection stood between them and the boardwalk. Within two minutes Rick found himself standing on the storied planks. He immediately moved to the rail. A nearly full moon hung low over the sea, its luminance shimmering milky flecks on the dark Atlantic. The boardwalk was alive with activity but the gentle and soothing noises of the surf could still be heard kissing the shadowy sand.

"Hey, this way," Vinny tugged at his sleeve.

Rick smiled and took a deep breath of the salt air that had assumed an enticing scent as it blended with the wonderful aroma of roasted peanuts wafting from a nearby stand.

The boards were a crowded affair. It seemed that the boardwalk was a great generational melting pot as people of all ages cruised in the pleasant night atmosphere. Some of the vacationers pursued a leisurely pace but amped-up children were also in abundance, urging their parents toward the spinning and undulating neon lights of the amusement piers tugging at them like an electromagnet.

It was not long before the friends came alongside "Fun Pier," the southernmost of the amusement venues. Rick had been able to identify the pier's Ferris wheel from some distance but he wondered at the large wooden building perched behind the twirling rides of the "Kiddieland" section. Vinny explained that the structure had once been the Convention Hall but now held a dark ride entitled "Spooks Hide-Away."

"Do those go out over the ocean?" Rick asked, pointing toward the bench seats of the "Ski Ride."

"Yeah they do. It's just like a ski lift," Vinny smiled, "except for the mountains, snow, and skis."

Rick marveled at the sights and sounds of the boardwalk. Hawkers tried their best to get the young men to throw balls into peach baskets or test their pitching skills by knocking over pins. But the pair ambled onward, immune to the barkers.

The bright lights of Marine Pier called to Rick, as his eyes traced the zipping cars of its Wild Mouse coaster racing around the towering metal track.

As they came abreast of Marine Pier, Rick noticed that it seemed to straddle the boardwalk. Suddenly a rumble echoed, followed by a chorus of screams. He hustled over to the inland rail in time to see The Jack Rabbit roller coaster speed by the sidewalk along Cedar Avenue.

"Hey. What's that?" Rick asked, pointing to the huge cylindrical structure rising from the roof of the building to their right.

"That's part of the Playland. It's the top of the carousel house."

Vinny nudged his friend forward but near the Kohr Bros. frozen custard stand he stopped again, staring at the cavernous entrance to the Casino Arcade in front of him.

"What's a scoota boat?" the excited young man asked, spying a sign for one of the Casino Arcade's rides.

"Like a bumper boat. You know, for kids."

Rick stepped in the direction of the entranceway. "Pig slide? What's a pig slide?" he queried after hearing two boys hustling toward the opening, discussing how they couldn't wait to get to the attraction.

"It's a crazy game. You throw a ball at a target and if you hit it, a trap door opens and a baby pig slides down a chute. You win if the pig goes into the hole that matches its name."

"Oh, I've got to see this," Rick laughed and began walking into the entranceway.

Vinny grabbed his friend by the arm. "Come on, there will be plenty of time for that kind of thing later. I promise we'll come back and tour all of the piers," he said in a pleading voice. "We've got to get to the Starlight." He dragged his pal from the Casino Arcade entrance. "We might not even get in if we don't hurry!"

As Rick turned he saw the façade of the ballroom and the line of teens and young adults waiting to enter. Although the Starlight was a popular spot all summer long, the presence of the Bandstand host had brought out a greater than average crowd. Needing no further urging he and Vinny jogged over the boards and joined the queue.

The line moved quickly and it wasn't long before they were inside the packed dance hall. The records were already spinning, as were the teens who twirled and bopped under the compulsion of the addictive rock and roll music.

Rick and Vinny were among the older members of the crowd. Unlike the two army buddies, most of those in attendance were too young to get into Wildwood's nightclubs so the Starlight provided the next best thing. Yet, the return of the now famous Dick Clark had brought many former teens to the ballroom to experience a wistful echo of their own teenage days.

"Hey, there he is," Rick fairly yelled in his friend's ear in order to be heard above The Silhouettes *Get a Job*. He pointed across the room to the stage where the Bandstand host stood sifting through a stack of 45s.

"Yup," Vinny nodded. "Hey, let's cut some rug," he slapped his pal on the back. "There are a lot of chicks here waiting for a pair like us."

Rick smiled. "Let's go. But head over there," he pointed to an area where it looked like the dancers were closer to their age, "too many ankle biters over this-a-way."

The young men had a great time dancing the night away. Dick Clark didn't disappoint and they not only swung a number of pretty girls around the floor but also joined in unison with the whole room to do The Madison and the Hully-Gully.

They were taking a breather, standing along one wall when Vinny announced that he was going to grab a drink. "You want something?" he asked his friend.

"No, I'm good," Rick replied distractedly, his eyes narrowing as he stared at something in the distance.

"Alright. I'll be back."

As Vinny headed off, Rick moved a bit to see around a couple who had begun to dance in front of him. His attention had been drawn to a portly man with a shock of gray hair. The man was on the edge of the stage and appeared quite agitated. The lenses of the man's dark-rimmed glasses gleamed in the reflected light of the mirrored ball that spun overhead. Rick slid between some dancers and moved closer. The gray-headed man had been met by an attendant but this seemed to aggravate him further and he began pushing the assistant backward, calling over his head to Dick Clark. Rick could not hear the man above the bombast of the music, but he could tell that he was yelling.

At first Clark didn't seem to notice the man but as he got more forceful with the attendant and closer to the DJ, the Bandstand host turned in his direction. Rick read Clark's face like a novel. Surprise, then irritation colored his features. He knew the man, and wasn't happy to see him. Clark turned to his left and said something to someone near the back of the stage. Two burly figures appeared and relieved the overmatched, back pedaling attendant. Each grabbed one of the intruder's arms and reversed his progress. The shock of gray hair bounced wildly as its owner appeared to raise his voice to a greater level, attempting to shout something at Dick Clark. The brawny guards easily dragged the invader from the stage and the trio disappeared through a swinging door.

The television personality wagged his head as if he were shaking off a bad dream and a moment later he was back to his charismatic self, leaning into the microphone to announce the next song.

Although the room was packed, few had noticed the event as they had been joyously occupied in their dancing. Those who had seen the antics of the gray-haired intruder thought little of the very brief display. But Rick rubbed his chin in contemplation. He had not been able to read the man's lips, but he had interpreted his body language. The man had been more than angry. He was frustrated. He was exasperated. Rick had dealt with such men before at his post in the army. This man displayed the same demeanor as one who... Rick would never finish the thought as Vinny popped up in front of him.

"Hey man, why'd you move? I had a heck of a time finding you!"

"Oh I just saw something and..."

Vinny cut him off. "Hey, there's that chick I was dancing with earlier! Who's that clown?" he quipped, pointing to a bi-speckled, lanky fellow dancing with a redheaded girl. "Can you believe that? Who does that four-eyed bean pole think he is?"

Rick recalled with some amusement how the girl had given Vinny the brush about a half an hour earlier and was amused even further at his friend's vexation that her smiling face indicated that she was having a great time with what Vinny considered a far inferior substitute.

"Here, hold this," Vinny said handing over his cup of soda.

Rick watched as his friend be-bopped his way across the floor. A grin spread over his face as he witnessed Vinny's attempts to draw the redhead's attention. Unfortunately, she seemed quite happy with her current beau. Vinny's annoyance began to mount. His ego blended with his Mediterranean blood. He simply couldn't believe that the object of his attention could prefer this fella over him! The young man from South Philly pulled out all of the stops, employing every dance move in his arsenal as he tried to divert the happy girl's eyes from her current partner. Finally, he forcibly interposed himself between the two. Rick took a step forward, anticipating that the tall boy might bring a fist down upon his friend's head.

It wasn't Vinny's rival who took action however. Much to his shock, the small Italian found himself being berated by the girl. Rick couldn't make out what she was saying, but her furrowed brows and wagging finger spoke volumes. A moment later the wounded and brooding young man had returned to Rick's side.

"So?" Rick smiled, handing back Vinny's drink.

"Oh, she's bats!"

"Didn't care for your dance steps, huh? Well, don't fret. For your birthday I'll get you some lessons at Arthur Murray's," he chuckled.

"Very funny. You're a laugh riot. Do you know what she called me?"

Rick couldn't wait to hear.

"Shorty. Shorty! Me!"

It was apparently lost on Vinny that not only did the girl's new partner tower about ten inches above him, but the redhead herself eclipsed him as well since the top of his head only reached the bottom of her chin.

Rick felt a tinge of empathy for his buddy and wrapped an arm around his shoulders. "Ah, forget her. I saw some pretty ones standing over this way just waiting to be asked onto the floor."

Although the affront to Vinny's pride hit him hard, the blow was easily softened as he found a number of other attractive partners. The pals were near exhaustion by the time the Bandstand host brought the evening to a close. The army buddies had had a wonderful time that they would long remember. Years later, even Vinny would laugh about the fiery redhead who had reamed him out the night Dick Clark had returned to the Starlight Ballroom.

As the friends filed out onto the boardwalk, "Yo Vin!" echoed above the amusement sounds as a dark-haired boy broke through the crowd.

"Hey, Joey! How's it going? Rick, this is a pal from the neighborhood, Joey. Joey, this is Rick, he's staying with me over at my Aunt Marie's."

The two new acquaintances exchanged greetings.

"Hey Vin, a lot of the old gang is here," he said. "We're going to grab a bite at the Tom Cat. Why don't you come along?"

"You hungry, Rick?" Vinny noticed the confusion on Rick's face. "The Tom Cat is a diner over on Rio Grande Avenue."

"Oh, sure," Rick nodded, recalling seeing the place as they entered the island that morning. "I could stand for some grub."

"Alright, sounds good," Vinny confirmed, turning back to Joey.

"A couple of the boys are fetching the cars. You can pile in," Joey said. "I've got to round up the girls. At the bathroom," he rolled his eyes. "You know how girls can't go five minutes without 'freshening up.' Meet me down at Oak and Atlantic."

Vinny led Rick off of the boardwalk and down the block. While they stood waiting, the music of a live band drifted from the restaurant/lounge of the hotel across the street.

"See that?" Vinny asked, pointing.

"What? The hotel?" Rick returned, peering at the brick frontage of the HofBrau Hotel.

"That, my friend is the birthplace of rock and roll."

"Sure," Rick said, giving his buddy a playful shove.

"No, it's true. That's where Bill Haley and the Comets first played *Rock Around the Clock*."

Rick shot Vinny a suspicious look but in gauging the expression on his companion's face, he reconsidered his disbelief. "Are you serious?"

"Absolutely. Haley and the Comets were the house band at the HofBrau and on Memorial Day weekend six years ago they debuted the song right there," he said, motioning toward the angled door of the hotel's lounge. "The song got countrywide exposure from being in that film, *The Blackboard Jungle*, but you're standing on hallowed ground, my friend. At least as far as rock and roll is concerned."

Rick was still contemplating the significance of the hotel across the way when Vinny's tap on the shoulder roused him.

"Here they come." He pointed to the ramp leading from the boardwalk where Joey's familiar face was seen with a quartet of girls.

"See Joyce, I told you that he was here," Joey said to one of the girls as they approached.

"Well if it isn't Joyce Sullivan," Vinny greeted a cute girl with light brown hair and the tiny freckles that so often decorate the noses of Irish girls.

"Hi there Vinny," she said, her smile telling a deeper story than her words.

"Joyce, this is my pal Rick. Rick, this is Joyce. And this is Lisa," he introduced a cute olive complected girl with black hair and eyes the color of onyx. "And this is Debbie, and... Hold the phone, is this little Pam?"

"You guessed it," Joey chimed in. "Debbie's little sister, is a lass of seventeen now." Had they not been identified as sisters it would not have taken much to figure it out.

39

Both girls had the same chestnut hair and hazel-green eyes. "Hey, here are the boys," Joey called out as a burgundy Hudson Hornet pulled to the curb followed closely by a yellow Mercury Monterey.

"Well open the door for the ladies," Vinny said to Rick but the young man was still staring into Lisa's dark eyes.

"Oh. Oh sure," Rick revived and followed orders.

The four girls climbed into the Hudson, driven by a boy named Mike who Rick met through the driver's side window. Rick, Joey and Vinny hustled into the Mercury where the newcomer was introduced to another of Vinny's neighborhood cronies, a fellow named Frank.

Even though it was late, the streets teemed with commotion. Cars cruised along Atlantic Avenue and people were still disappearing into the night clubs; the excellent music of the live acts escaping each time a door opened.

Despite the happy tumult that made the streets buzz with activity it didn't take long to cover the fourteen blocks south to Rio Grande Avenue. As they drove westward on the city's main entranceway Rick easily spotted their destination. Red letters on a white placard announced that this was indeed the Tom Cat diner, should a visitor be too daft to gather as much from the huge black cat marquee.

The place was obviously a popular one as it was hopping despite its distance from the boardwalk and clubs. Luckily, two empty tables were found and when pushed together were able to accommodate the group of four girls and five boys.

Ten cent sodas were ordered all around and while the girls mostly requested a slice of cake for an additional dime, the boys seemed a bit more ravenous, opting to go the twenty-five cents for a sandwich.

The old friends chatted noisily, recalling tales from their collective youth running the streets of South Philadelphia as well as those wonderful summer weekends they had often shared in the Wildwoods. One of the parties however seemed reluctant to participate fully. Lisa smiled and added comments when asked, but there was a reserved, withdrawn quality that did not escape Rick's eye. The young man was far from displeased at this fact since it gave him an opportunity to speak with her outside of the nostalgic camaraderie of which he really could not contribute. Still, he wondered what could be bothering her.

"So you went to high school with Vinny?" Rick asked the pretty, tanned girl across the table.

"Yes. We all attended Southern," Lisa replied in a quiet, though sweet voice.

"Are you in Wildwood for the weekend?"

"No, I'm working down here all summer. I'm a chambermaid over at the 24th Street Motel. Joyce's grandmother has a little place on Leaming Ave and is letting us stay as long as we do chores and pay for food."

"Oh," he said, admiring her sparkling, dark eyes. "And what do you do in the off season?"

"I'm in school. At Temple University. I'm studying nursing." She smiled demurely. "And how did you hook up with Vinny?"

He laughed. "We were in the army together."

"Is that right?" the girl's voice was quiet, but polite. "Were you a clerk too? I know that was Vince's job." Her dainty lips wrapped around the straw protruding from her cherry Coke.

"No. I was an M.P. Vinny and I were in the same office, but I was an investigator."

Rick saw the brown liquid suddenly descend from the straw as the pretty lips abruptly released the plastic. Lisa seemed to gasp in surprise at Rick's revelation.

"An investigator? Like a detective?" the girl asked in a subdued voice.

He chuckled. "Well not exactly. Mostly I tracked down guys who had gone AWOL."

Her mouth opened, as if to say something but it closed again and a troubled expression crossed her face. Her lips parted once more but Mike suddenly cut her off.

"Hey Rick! Did Vinny ever tell you about the time he and Joey snuck into Connie Mack Stadium?"

"Aw, don't tell him that one!" Vinny bemoaned.

Mike didn't heed the order however and a comical tale followed describing how in their mid-teens the two friends had conned their way into the bowels of the sports arena during a Phillies game by pretending to be part of the janitorial crew. The pair were elated that they got past the gate and figured that they were going to end up with front row seats for the contest. Unfortunately they became ensnared in their own lie and ended up scrubbing urinals in the visiting team's locker room.

"Hey, I got Duke Snider's autograph didn't I?" Vinny chimed in.

"Sure, on a roll of toilet paper!" Mike added, laughing so hard that he nearly choked on his bacon and lettuce sandwich.

That night Rick lay in bed staring up at the ceiling. He couldn't stop thinking about the pretty Italian girl he had met. He hoped that he would see more of her. But he also wondered about that concerned expression that clouded her face and what she was about to say before the conversation had shifted in other directions.

Fun Pier

43

Marine Pier
Photos courtesy of the Wildwood Historical Society

Casino Arcade Entrance
Photo courtesy of the Wildwood Historical Society

Starlight Ballroom
Photo courtesy of the Wildwood Historical Society

Dick Clark at the Starlight Ballroom
Photos courtesy of the Wildwood Historical Society

The HofBrau Hotel

Photo courtesy of the Wildwood Historical Society

The Tom Cat Diner

Photo courtesy of the Wildwood Historical Society

Chapter 4

The next morning dawned bright and cloudless. "What's so funny?" Rick groggily asked, sitting up in bed. It took him a moment to realize that it wasn't Vinny laughing, but rather the cackling cry of a seagull perched somewhere beyond the open window.

The young men's army timetable had not abandoned them and despite their late night they were out of bed and dressed at an early hour. Rick and Vinny decided to spend the morning tackling the faded portion of the wall of the main house. After a hasty breakfast they made a quick trip over to the corner of Bennett and Pacific where the proprietor of Dewey Wallpaper and Paint outfitted them with a gallon of the proper hue as well as some of the hardware that they found lacking in the shed.

The workers methodically set up their ladder and developed an efficient system where they would take shifts painting while the other would stay on the ground, reapplying the roller and handling any assisting tasks that needed to be undertaken.

By ten o'clock the tenants of The Holly Beach House began their procession toward the beach. The couple in Unit #1 bid them a happy good morning as they headed out for their day in the sun. The young man who worked on the fishing boat had left the rooming house much earlier but the three teenage fellows whose jobs were on the boardwalk scurried down the back stairs, raucously jostling one another as they each grabbed a towel from the line and hustled up Burk Avenue on their way to the beach.

Pop! Pop! Pop! snapped from behind Rick as he bent to run the roller in the tray.

"Hey there Marshal," he said, turning to the bronze skinned, sandy-haired seven-year-old who was pointing his cap pistol at him. "You didn't have to go and plug me. I would've come along peacefully."

"Oh, Jackie!" a woman wearing a wide brimmed hat and dark glasses called, stepping from the screen door of Unit #2. "Leave those boys alone. Come along now; give your father a hand."

A man with tinted lenses clipped over his normal eyeglasses and a nose streaked with zinc-oxide appeared from behind the station wagon parked in the driveway. The poor fellow was encumbered with so many accoutrements that it appeared as if he was leaving for an expedition to scale Kilimanjaro. Upon closer inspection however, it became apparent that his gear was specifically outfitted for a day at the beach. Amongst his paraphernalia were three folding aluminum chairs precariously held in his hands and an immense canvas bag over one shoulder. A green and white umbrella was uncomfortably pinioned under an arm and the transistor radio that dangled from a cord around his neck swung wildly as he gingerly waddled up the drive.

"Marge, I don't see what help Jackie is going to be, but you could grab one of these chairs for me."

"Oh, of course dear. I'm sorry." The woman tugged at the plaid webbing, sliding the chair from her husband's grip. He released the other chair in the same hand and leaned it against his leg as he flexed his fist repeatedly, trying to work out a cramp before picking it back up.

"Your turn," Vinny said as he stepped from the ladder onto the pavement. "Hold on a minute," he tapped Rick on the shoulder as he spied the beleaguered father. "I'll be

49

right back." Vinny hustled down the drive and disappeared into the kitchen door. Rick could hear voices and a moment later his friend was back in sight.

"Hey Mr. Owens!" Vinny called. "I think I can help. Wait there."

The painter disappeared around the back corner of the house. Banging and shuffling reverberated from inside the shed before Vinny returned carrying something.

"Here you go! This ought to do the trick." He produced a three foot frame of stiff, wire-like aluminum with two wheels on the bottom. The gizmo was not an uncommon one in urban settings where elderly ladies did their shopping at neighborhood groceries. The frame pulled open to form a basket, the handle extending beyond the basket so that the apparatus could be tilted forward and pulled along on its wheels.

"Now that's a good idea!" Mr. Owens commended. He slid the umbrella into the basket and pushed the canvas bag in alongside it. The radio found a home atop the bag. The bottom support of the two chairs he held slipped nicely over the handle. "Oh, this is going to make things a lot easier," he said, wiping his brow. "Thanks!"

"Oh, let me pull it!" Jackie said, grabbing the handle.

"Even better," the father smiled at Vinny.

In another minute the happy family was out of sight, en route to a splendid day on the wide sands of Wildwood's beach.

"I saw that thing in the shed earlier. I had to ask Aunt Marie if she minded me loaning it to them," Vinny reported.

"Some pretty nifty thinking," Rick said, dipping the roller.

Vinny rubbed his chin. "Only... If it were a little lighter... plastic wheels maybe. And folded in half, for easier storage. ...Maybe netting instead of that rigid basket," he pondered. Vinny shrugged his shoulders. "Ah! I'll have to give that some more thought one day. I might be able to make a million dollars! Here you are," he said, shifting back to the task at hand.

"Thanks," Rick replied, taking the roller and starting up the ladder.

Before noon the friends were on the beach. Rather than head surfside at Burk Avenue however, they had turned south once on the boardwalk and trekked the five blocks to Hand Avenue, which was where those from Vinny's neighborhood hung out.

There were a great many people on the beach but the expanse was so wide, "crowded" would not be a fitting adjective. The ample space meant that parties could easily spread themselves apart from their neighbors. It did not take long before they found the blankets of the group they had been with at the Tom Cat. Vinny and Rick quickly pulled the towels from around their necks and stretched them on the powdery, white sand. Their shirts were quickly stripped and the few bucks from their pockets were tucked in the toe of their sneakers, although it took Rick several tries to get his hand under the tongue of his shoe as he couldn't take his eyes from the petite girl he had met the night before; the two piece swimsuit she wore distracting the young man beyond reason.

"Heh, that's pretty cool!" Rick said.

"What?"

"That!" he pointed to the gray and red Piper Cub slowly droning in a northerly direction a thousand yards out over the ocean.

"You've never seen a banner plane? It won't be the last one you see; not in Wildwood anyway. It's better advertising than TV. On the beach, you can't turn the channel-- and the audience is targeted. Vacationers want to know where to eat and where to buy their suntan oil. Hey, let's go for a quick dip," Vinny said, slapping his friend on the arm.

"Ok," Rick assented. They took off toward the surf, dashing past the white wooden stand and the red shirted lifeguard perched atop it.

Rick was a strong swimmer, but he had never actually been in the ocean before. At first he found the turbulent nature of the waves and tide a bit unnerving, but it didn't take him long to get used to the sensation of the disorderly churning. In fact, once Vinny had taught him how to body surf, it was difficult to get the newcomer to agree to leave the water.

"Did you forget about a certain young lady sunning herself over yonder?" Vinny goaded after three quarters of an hour had elapsed.

Rick had been having such a blast that he *had* in fact forgotten all about Lisa. His pal's reminder caused him to suddenly jerk his head westward. He squinted and shaded his eyes, in an effort to make sure the pretty girl was still on the beach. Vinny laughed uproariously at his friend's abrupt realization. The young men paid for their inattentiveness when a massive wave smacked both squarely in the back, sending them sprawling head first into the bubbling foam. Rick helplessly tumbled like a ragdoll, moments later finding himself slumped in inches of water as the surf retreated.

Rick opened one eye to find his buddy next to him, also resembling the survivor of a shipwreck. The two shared a laugh over their ordeal before hauling themselves off of the wet sand and back up to their friends.

Rick and Vinny flopped onto their towels and the warm, inviting rays, unimpeded by even a single cloud, dried the pair within minutes. Only their hair and swim trunks could hold onto the moisture for any duration.

The DJs at Wibbage, or "The Good Guys" as WIBG's disc jockeys were collectively called, kept the South Philly kids company on the beach, their transistor radio delivering an endless supply of rock and roll hits.

After some playful conversation amongst the whole group, Rick and Vinny dug into the brown paper bag they had brought along. In short order they had reduced a pair of ham and cheese sandwiches to crumbs. Thankfully the girls generously offered some lemonade from the jug they had with them as the friends had forgotten to bring any liquid refreshment of their own.

Joyce was able to coax Vinny into the game the others were playing with a large inflatable beach ball, leaving Rick lounging alone with Lisa.

"So are you working? Now that you're out of the army, I mean."

"I've got a job at the A&P back home, but I'm set up to start school at Ohio State on the G.I. Bill as soon as summer is over."

"Oh, that's right; you're from Ohio aren't you."

"Yup. But I'll tell you," Rick propped himself up on his elbow. "I think the coast is getting a hold on me. Weekends in my town are spent at a community pool. This..." he said, staring off at the vastness of the blue Atlantic. "...This I could get used to."

The corners of Lisa's small, attractive mouth lifted, as if to say that she would welcome such a circumstance. The smile faded quickly though, and a more serious expression laid claim to her pretty features. She lifted her sunglasses, revealing those glistening dark eyes. "Rick... Can I ask you something? I mean, you can say no. Don't feel that you have to..."

"What is it?"

"Well..." Her mouth took a pouty, somber turn which despite its gravity, was no less becoming. "My cousin Johnny has disappeared."

"Disappeared?"

She nodded solemnly. "He was here, in Wildwood, but no one has heard from him in two days." She continued, "The police have been told. So have the newspapers. But nobody seems to be taking it seriously."

Rick's brow furrowed. "The newspapers? If the police aren't taking his disappearance seriously, why would they notify the papers?"

"Oh, the police didn't go to the papers. It was Johnny's manager."

"His manager?"

"Yes," the tanned girl sat up. "Johnny is a singer. His real name is Johnny Tatorini but he goes by Johnny Taylor."

"Johnny Taylor..." Rick rubbed his chin. "I've never heard of him."

"He's trying to break in. He's done some small engagements in Philadelphia and he and his Uncle Rudy, that's his manager, were down here trying to get him booked in the clubs." Lisa sighed. "I'm really worried about him. Johnny's only nineteen. He would never go off on his own someplace..." her words trailed away.

"Two days isn't really long enough for the police to take much notice," Rick advised.

"Would you look into it?" Lisa blurted, finally expelling the idea she had been laboring to express.

"Me?"

"Yes, you said that you were a Military Policeman," she hurriedly stated as she leaned forward, a hopeful optimism coating her words. "That's what you did, right? You found missing men!"

"Well," he rubbed at the back of his neck. "Kind of..." Rick didn't really believe that anything nefarious could have happened to Lisa's cousin. He surmised that she was overreacting; a kind girl driven more by loving concern than true suspicion. In pondering the situation he saw no harm, and only benefit in pledging aid to a girl whose devotion he would so like to acquire. "He'll turn up in short order on his own anyhow," Rick thought to himself. "Ok. Sure," he said. "I'll see what I can find out. If," he continued, looking sheepishly into her stunning eyes. "You promise to make a date with me."

Her smile answered before the words passed her lips.

"So tonight we're going to the boardwalk with Lisa and Joyce," Rick called over the divider in the outdoor shower stall.

"Oh, is that right?" Vinny replied above the sound of the cascade gushing from the nozzle over his head.

"Oh, don't act like you object," Rick returned, leaning back to rinse the shampoo from his hair. "You and Joyce seem to be getting on nicely. I suspect a glowing ember has reignited."

Vinny smiled to himself but made no reply.

"So, we pick the girls up at Joyce's grandmom's place over on Leaming," Rick continued, spinning the shower knobs to the "off" position. "Lisa says we can park at the motel where she works; it's close to the amusement piers."

"24th Street, right?" Vinny asked, cutting off the flow in his own stall.

"Yup."

"What time?" Vinny asked, grabbing the towel that hung over the wooden door.

"Seven."

———————————

"What can you tell me about Lisa's cousin Johnny?" Rick asked as the Chevy cruised along Pacific Avenue.

"Nice enough fella. I can't imagine why he'd go missing."

"Can he sing?" Rick posed, the velvety voices of the Everly Brothers' *Bye Bye Love* playing on the radio prompting the question.

Vinny shrugged. "Yeah, I guess. I heard him do a couple of numbers at a block party this past spring. He's a bit late though."

"How's that?"

"Frankie Avalon, Bobby Rydell, Fabian... the market's a little flooded with singers of Italian extraction out of South Philly."

Rick nodded mildly as he considered Vinny's comments. "What do the rest of your friends think about him disappearing?"

"They pretty much laughed it off. Lisa brought him around but he's not part of our crowd and no one really knows him. So you think you can find him?"

It was Rick's turn to shrug. "I think he'll turn up on his own but I promised I'd look into it."

"Well, she's got a good man on the case," Vinny gave him a soft punch on the arm. "You certainly tracked down plenty of G.I.s. I hope knowing you're on the job will keep that frown off of her face."

"She promised me she'll put it out of her head and have fun tonight."

The tires of the red and white Bel Air rolled up the two concrete strips that served as a driveway for the small cottage on the west end of Leaming Ave. Vinny gave the horn a soft toot that oddly seemed in tune with the Drifters *Dance With Me* emanating from the car's speakers. The screen door swung open and the two pretty girls stepped out, each wearing a light dress featuring a seasonal print.

Rick hopped from the car and folded the seat forward. He extended a hand to help Lisa into the rear seat of the convertible. His date slid across and he dropped in beside her, pulling the seat back so that Joyce could assume her place next to the driver.

The streets were busy, not just with automobiles, but also with the mass exodus of pedestrians all headed easterly toward the boardwalk. It seemed that each and every intersection held more vacationers than the traffic lights could accommodate. To his credit, again and again Vinny patiently waved on those who had been unable to make the crossing before the light had changed.

Vinny turned the Chevy onto 26th Street and headed in the direction of the beach. At Surf Avenue, he made a left. Rick sat up a bit in his seat, intrigued by a red and orange glow up ahead. As they got closer he realized that it was a neon facsimile of a flickering torch, marking a motel on 23rd Street called *The Flame Inn*.

"Wow, look at the size of that place," Rick said, spying another motel, *The Thunderbird Inn*.

"Yeah, it's got a huge pool in the courtyard too," Vinny explained.

Across the street, Rick spied a vertical neon "MOTEL" sign. A smaller script near the "O" read "24th St." Vinny swung the Chevy into an open space at the brownish-red motel. "Here ok?" he asked over his shoulder to Lisa.

"I think so," she said. "I have to drop off a key. I'll make sure that this spot is alright."

Rick accompanied Lisa to the office where a young man sat behind the counter humming a tune, his pencil scratching potential lyrics under the staff that lined the paper.

"Hello, Mel."

"Oh, hi ya Lisa."

"I brought back the key to 22," she said, dropping it atop the manuscript paper. "I found it on the ground by the pool today and forgot all about it."

"Ok, thanks," he said, hanging the key in its proper place on a numbered grid of hooks.

"We're headed up to the boards. Are we okay parked there?" Lisa asked, pointing to the convertible Bel Air.

Mel leaned over the counter. "Yeah, sure. That's fine."

"Alright then, catch you later."

"Have fun."

58

"What's that guy another aspiring musician?" Rick asked as they walked away.

Lisa laughed. "Well not exactly. He's an *aspiring songwriter*. I'm afraid he's been annoying one of the guests too," she added, knitting her brows.

"How so?"

"Well, we've got Irving Shapiro staying in #11. He's composed a number of hits. Mel keeps trying to pick his brain."

"Irving Shapiro? What hits has he written? I've never heard of him."

Lisa smiled. "Actually I couldn't tell you," she chuckled. "Mel said that he uses different pen names. He said that the managers of artists prefer it that way so that it doesn't look like one man is the key to the success of so many singers." As they reached the convertible she said to Vinny, "The car is fine here."

"Great. Let's go." He shot out his elbow, inviting Joyce's hand into the crook. The girl's tiny freckled nose crinkled as she smiled approvingly.

"Hey you know, I promised your brother I'd check out that coaster... what was it called? *The Flyer*?"

"That's right," Vinny confirmed as they crossed Surf Avenue. "Let's head over to Hunt's Pier. That's where The Flyer is. I heard that they've got a couple of new rides on Hunt's and I said that I'd let Georgie know about any new attractions."

Once on the boards the double daters turned south. Rick's vision was transfixed on the pier up ahead where twinkling lights rimmed the rails of The Flyer's white framing. His eyes traced the form of a train race down a decline and faint screams could be heard by the thrilled riders.

Suddenly Vinny grabbed hold of his distracted friend's arm and tugged him from the concrete slab he was walking upon.

"I'd stay off of the cement," Vinny said, nodding behind them. Rick turned to see a yellow car humming toward them toting another six carriages behind it.

"Now there's an innovative idea," Rick said, reading the word "Sightseer" painted in blue upon the passing tram.

"They're from the '39 World's Fair," Vinny informed.

"No foolin'?"

"No foolin. They've been used here for ten years or so. I've never ridden on one, as I've always been a fit lad but the boardwalk is two miles long, so it's a nice option for the less vigorous."

As the couples ambled toward Hunt's Pier a burly man in a dark suit leaned against a pole outside of the 24th Street Motel. He pushed his fedora up a bit and touched his lighter to the cigarette held between his lips. He exhaled, peering through the cloud of smoke as he kept a watchful eye on room # 11.

The 24th St. Motel

Photo courtesy of the Wildwood Historical Society

Chapter 5

"The Flyer" Rick said to himself, as he gazed up at the red glowing letters that sat atop the coaster's curved loading platform at the front of the pier. The platform's fascia boldly stated "Thrilling Ride Over the Ocean."

"This way," Vinny urged, diverting the newcomer from the roller coaster. "The ticket booth is over here."

As they waited in line for tickets, Rick read a sign that adorned a rotating cube atop a pole. It described Hunt's Pier as "an Oceanic Wonderland." He looked around at the many rides rolling, spinning, and swooping around him and smiled a confirmation of the sign's boast.

"Have you girls been on the Golden Nugget yet?" asked Vinny as the boys returned with booklets of tickets.

"I haven't," Joyce replied. "How about you, Lisa?"

"No, I haven't either."

"The Golden Nugget? I'm guessing it's that giant mountain-looking thing back that-away?" Rick pointed to the orange faux structure meant to resemble a geological feature of the country's southwest.

"Yeah, that it. It's a new ride, just opened this year. I heard it's like a dark-ride/roller coaster combination," Vinny reported.

"Sounds cool."

"How about we start near the front of the pier and work our way back. The Golden Nugget can be our grand finale."

The others agreed with Vinny's plan and all headed over to join the line waiting to ride The Flyer. It didn't take long before they were seated in one of the train's four cars each of which conveniently held four people.

Rick and Lisa were lucky enough to be assigned to the front seats in the first car. The operator released the long wooden handle and they were soon climbing the lift hill, the clickity-clack of the gear chain pulling them aloft. A painted sign on one of the cross-members warned to "Hold Your Hats."

The car continued its ascent. At the crest, white lights danced around a sign where "Hunt's Pier" was painted in red letters. As they reached the summit a second of anticipation fluttered in their stomachs and then the car roared down the other side. Lisa let out a subdued scream as she gripped Rick's hand.

The coaster sped by the Mini Hot Rods where young children toured the fairy tale scenes that decorated the area encircled by The Flyer's wooden superstructure.

Rick's hair blew back as the car zoomed around the distant turn at the rear of the pier, nearly cruising over the Atlantic itself. As the train returned toward the boardwalk, a number of shallow dips and turns slowed the cars before they docked back at the station. Expressions of delight ornamented the faces of those eagerly awaiting their turn on the coaster.

The two couples climbing from The Flyer grinned happily as they descended back down to the concrete of the pier.

"Hey!" Rick called out, dragging Lisa by the hand.

"Where are you going?" a confused Vinny asked, as he and Joyce hurried to keep up.

"How cool!" Rick blurted, admiring the detail on the facsimile of the Pennsylvania Railroad locomotive cruising past as it carried a train-load of small children on a ride around the perimeter of The Flyer's track.

Vinny laughed. "Oh yeah, Lisa. I should've told you that Romeo here is a train nut. Come on," he pulled his pal from the kiddie attraction.

The friends had a blast on the "Crazy Cups," "Tilt-a-Shell," and the "Scrambler," before Vinny looked seriously into Joyce's eyes and asked, "Are you brave enough for a journey into the darkest reaches of Africa?"

The girl's freckled nose crinkled into a smile. "I think so," she chuckled.

"Off to Jungleland then!" her date commanded, leading the group across the pier.

The Jungleland ride had been a new addition to the pier the previous year and had quickly become a favorite in the Wildwoods. Thousands came to the island to escape to the Jersey shore but the Jungleland attraction took them even further, on an exploration of the mysterious rivers of the "dark continent."

"Pretty neat!" Rick commented upon seeing the exterior of the attraction. Bamboo and thatch matting, rough timbers brightly painted in African patterns, and a trio of peak-roofed huts fronted the ride. A robotic native sat atop the covered entranceway, rhythmically banging away on a tribal drum.

As they waited in the line, Rick smiled as he read over a series of signs describing the ride: "See the Mad Witch Doctor," "See the Elephants at the Watering Hole," "See What Happens to the Stray Missionaries," "See the Fight to the Death between a Native Boy & Croc." He had no sooner finished reading and they were boarding a reproduction river steamer named the *Swamp Lilly*.

Another ten riders piled in before the "guide" signaled the craft forward.

Rick thought that the ride was a hoot. The guide was a kaki-clad man who made liberal use of a microphone, as he described a series of scenes on the "expedition to find the lost missionaries." Mechanical monkeys, crocodiles, and snakes populated the river-way as did a charging rhino. The guide even fired blanks from a revolver as a rampaging hippo "attacked" the boat.

Unfriendly, cannibalistic natives were also among the robotic inhabitants of this jungle. The boat eventually headed into a cave where some dark ride staples were used, albeit in a rain forest context. Lisa clung tightly to his arm as the *Swamp Lilly* approached a waterfall pouring its contents in the boat's path. Lisa and Joyce fretted over the impending dousing, alternating between gasps and squeals. Suddenly the flow stopped, and each girl's hair-do avoided calamity.

"Ha!" laughed Rick as they exited the boat. "I never thought I'd get to go to Africa! Now I can cross that off of my list," he smiled.

Next they headed toward the newest attraction on the pier, the massive structure of the Golden Nugget mine ride.

The ride was housed in the huge mountainesque edifice that looked like a giant earthen-toned iceberg. The green spikes of artificial cacti cresting the roofline foretold that the ride took passengers up to the pinnacle of the structure. As they approached, a mine-car filled with tourists rattled above them, as it left a timber-braced shaft-opening only to reenter the mountain moments later through a similar portal.

"Hey, this is pretty cool," Vinny said as he admired the façade that fronted the loading platform. "Look, they've got a saloon... a bank... a barber shop..." he pointed toward each of the make-believe establishments from an old west town. "I feel like I'm in Dodge City!"

The foursome handed over their tickets and an attendant in authentic looking western attire instructed them to climb aboard a coaster carriage made out to resemble a mine-car. As their vehicle started forward, Vinny's smile was even brighter than on the previous rides as he relished his first experience on the new attraction.

The car climbed a hill that skirted the outside of the mountain before disappearing into a gaping hole marked "Golden Nugget Shaft." They then ascended a second hill that rimmed the side of the ride. As their path took them past two jagged openings on their right, they could see the lights of Marine Pier twinkling to the south. Just before the car reached the top of the structure, Rick caught a brief glimpse of the vast Atlantic, the moon tracing a glistening river-like trail up to the breakers.

Upon reaching the roof of the ride, the mine-car rattled a twisting path through a shallow chasm. When they emerged from the gulch, they were facing west and were favored with a view of the electric brilliance of the boardwalk. The flashing white lights of The Flyer danced off to their right.

Atop the ride, they were treated to a number of sights that personified the old west theme: cowboys, Indians, a covered wagon, a gold prospector, and a graveyard modeled after the famous "Boot Hill." As they snaked through the motif, the mood was enhanced as sounds fitting the frontier setting seeped from hidden speakers. Lisa gasped as they approached the skeletal remains of a cowboy astride an equally skeletal horse. An arrow protruding from the unfortunate rider's ribcage, declared the means of his demise.

As the car swung past the long expired cowboy, they progressed toward an opening alarmingly marked as a "bottomless shaft." The girls screamed as the car plunged into the hole. Although the drop had not been a long one, the anticipation and the darkness made it feel much more threatening.

Now they were inside the mountain where the ride combined the drops and turns of a coaster with many of the gimmicks used in more traditional "dark rides." A spooky soundtrack of howling winds and creaking timber accompanied them through the murky interior. Here the couples experienced animatronic miners intent on dynamiting their way to wealth as well a stack of barrels that seemed as if they would topple onto them. They were menaced by both a giant spider and an attacking wolf and their senses confused when they passed through a spinning tunnel. The girls were more stoic when they encountered a repeat of the waterfall gag they had survived in Jungleland. The couples crossed the path of a few more skeletons before their "runaway" mine-car pulled back into the loading area.

"Oh man," Vinny smiled, piling onto the platform. "Is my brother going to love this one! Remind me to get a postcard with this ride on it and send it to him. He'll go nuts itching to get down here," he devilishly added. "Who's up for some miniature golf?" he asked, as he led the way toward the front of the pier.

———————————

Unhappy with his latest effort, Mel crumbled the page and dropped it into the trash can but the balled up paper rolled from the overflowing bin onto the floor. With a sigh, the clerk retrieved the discarded song and grabbed hold of the tin wastepaper basket. He walked the receptacle around back, emptying the refuse into one of the larger metal cans kept out of the view of the guests. Mel returned to the office and as he dropped the can back into place, he noticed a note on the countertop.

"Please bring some towels to room 11," he read aloud. He smiled. "Maybe Mr. Shapiro will have a few minutes to chat," he mumbled to himself. He left the counter and vanished through a swinging door. A minute later he reappeared with a short stack of towels and exited the office. The young man followed the bright yellow, triangular patterned iron railing until he reached #11. Three white diagonal wooden appliqués decorated the door and Mel rapped in the center of the top diamond.

A solid ten seconds passed and Mel knocked again, calling: "Mr. Shapiro?" through the one inch crack of the ajar door. The thin hand of his watch had swept a quarter of the way around its face when the attentive young man nudged open the door and poked his head inside.

"Mr. Shapiro, I have your towels." The would-be songwriter stole a glance around the interior, his eyes widening at the dozen pages of composition paper piled atop the round table beside a small electric piano. Compulsively, he entered further. Placing the towels on the surface, he lifted the music and began paging through the compositions, his lustful curiosity eclipsing his manners. Mel stepped leftward for better light. When he cleared the end of the two beds, his eyes drifted past the page to spy a pair of naked, twisted legs protruding across the bathroom threshold.

The stunned young man rushed across the room, the music still in his hand. "Mr. Shapiro! Mr. Shapiro!" He bent low and spoke down into the ashen face of the elderly man. "Are you alright?" He took the index and middle finger of his free hand and touched them to the songwriter's neck. He did not feel a pulse. Rising, he quickly darted from the room. Upon exiting however, his path was impeded as he collided with a sturdy, brawny frame. Looking up into the dark-suited man's face, Mel realized that he had seen him before. About an hour prior, the man had been in Irving Shapiro's room and raised voices had reverberated from #11 before the large man had left in a huff.

"Where are you goin', pal?" the gravelly voice asked.

"What? Mr. Shapiro-- something's happened to him! We need to get help!"

"Something happened to him, eh?" The flat-nosed man nonchalantly took a drag from his cigarette. "And here you are running from the room with a guilty look on your face."

"Guilty? What?"

He adjusted his gray fedora. "What's that you've got there in your hand? I don't know if you killed the guy; but you're certainly stealin' from him."

The blood drained from Mel's face.

"Tell you what. Hand over that music and I'll be on my way. I won't say nothin'."

The young man's eyes widened with fright. He pushed his way around the man and began hurriedly walking up the street, desperate to put space between himself and his accuser. He should have rushed straight for the phone in the office but fear and alarm played havoc with his reason.

68

He turned right on Surf Avenue. Glancing over his shoulder a sense of dread gripped him when he saw the man in the dark suit walking calmly, but briskly behind him. He was two steps into a run and then immediately slowed again to a fast walk.

"No, I can't run," he thought. "It will make me look guilty!" As he hurried onward, his mind raced. He hadn't done anything wrong! The police would believe him! Or would they? Hyper-anxiety sent him into senselessness. Did the man behind him kill the composer? Had he been waiting to pin it on the first person who entered the room? Did Mr. Shapiro even write that note? His paranoia grew.

Four blocks later and the man was still behind him. "The boardwalk. I'll lose him in the crowd," he thought, his wild eyes fixating on the ramp ahead. As he reached the boards he turned and looked. The man was still coming. Suddenly he felt the papers in his hand. "He wants these," he thought. "I could give them to him. He said he'd leave me alone if I handed them over... No," his opinion suddenly turned on a dime. "If he did kill Mr. Shapiro, once he has these, I'd have no leverage! He'd be free to say that I'm the murderer!" He folded the pages and slipped them into his back pocket.

"The pier," he thought. "It will be packed with people. I'll be able to lose him more easily on the pier." A rational mind would have shunned such a maneuver, fearing being boxed in but the clerk was hardly thinking clearly. Mel walked past The Flyer and weaved into the crowd. He headed deeper, past the Roto-Jets. He threaded his way to the boarding platform of the huge orange-brown mine ride toward the rear of the pier. Ducking around its far corner he peered out over the railing of the mock western town. He did not see his pursuer. A wave of relief swept over him. Leaving his nook, he retraced his steps in a determined effort to make it back to the boardwalk. As he came abreast of Jungleland, his heart dropped. Some hundred feet to his left his antagonist's head rose above the crowd as the big man climbed upon a bench for a better view. Mel ducked into the throng near the jungle ride's entrance, disappearing momentarily.

He peeked around a fake palm. A sudden shock of panic jolted the unfortunate clerk. The man was making a beeline straight for him! Mel took off again, resuming his brisk pace. He fled back toward the boardwalk. The frightened motel worker turned and saw that his chaser was gaining. The flat-nosed man in the dark suit had quickened his step. As he left the pier he glanced back again. The hunter was even nearer! The fear-ridden young man kept peering over his shoulder as he continued onward, stumbling right into the path of the tram car. The electric powered vehicle's top speed was only 5 miles-per-hour, but the grille slammed the inattentive clerk full upon his thighs and midsection, throwing him from his feet. Mel landed upon his backside, his momentum causing the rear of his head to slam onto the cement pathway upon which the tram ran.

"Oh, man. That guy just got clobbered," Vinny announced. However his report was unnecessary as all four in his party had seen the accident. Lisa took off at a run, trailed by the others.

"I'm a nursing student," she stated. "Please get back. Go and call for an ambulance," she ordered a by-stander who quickly vanished to follow her instructions.

"Hey, that's the fellow from your motel, Lisa!" Joyce stated but the dutiful future nurse made no comment as she surveyed the injury of the unconscious clerk.

"Rick, go and grab some beach towels," she said, pointing toward a nearby vendor.

He returned in a flash and with extreme care, Lisa applied a folded towel to the gaping wound at the back of Mel's head. Suddenly the clerk's eyes shot open and rolled wildly.

"You're alright," Lisa soothed. "But don't move. We've called for an ambulance. Just lie still. Soon you'll be under a doctor's care."

Mel gasped. He tried to speak and hoarsely blurted "Which doctor..."

Lisa maintained her calm. "Don't you worry. The attending physician will be top notch. I promise." The young man's eyes fluttered and he slipped from consciousness.

Two policemen hustled up and the young lady turned the first-aid operation over to them. "He has a fractured skull," she informed the officers. "Be very careful."

"I knew this would happen," a pretty girl in the crowd declared as she peered at the injured man.

"Oh Floss!" her friend returned, gasping at the amount of blood on the boardwalk.

"No. I mean it. If it were up to me, the tram-car would have an announcement. You know, one that could be used to warn people who might be in the way. It should say something like: Watch the..."

The young lady's words were lost to the group as the wail of a siren suddenly pierced the boardwalk sounds. "Here they come now," one of the policemen said.

Note: The famous tram car warning voiced by Floss Stingel was added in 1971.

Photos courtesy of the Wildwood Historical Society

SEE
THE WITCH DOCTOR

SEE
THE ELEPHANT
AT THE WATER HOLE

SEE
SNAPPING
CROCS.

SEE
MISSIONAIRES

SEE
THE FLOWERED JUNGLE

SEE
NATIVE BOY & CROC.

SEE
FRIENDLY HIPPOS

Jungleland
Photos courtesy of the Wildwood Historical Society

The Golden Nugget
Photo courtesy of the Wildwood Historical Society

Hunt's Pier
Photo courtesy of the Wildwood Historical Society

74

Chapter 6

"Well," Vinny said as the ambulance disappeared out of sight. "Are we still going to play some miniature golf?" he asked, peering aloft at the huge sign reading "Ocean Center Skyline Golf."

Lisa was pensive.   "I think we should go back to the motel. It doesn't make sense for Mel to have been up here. I wonder who's minding the store."

The others agreed, hoping to put Lisa at ease. They headed north back toward 24th Street.   As they were passing 22nd Street they nearly collided with Vinny's pal Joey and Connie, a girl from the crowd Rick had met at the beach.

"Yo Vin! What are youse guys up to?" Joey asked.

Vinny answered for the group. "We were leaving Hunt's Pier and we saw the clerk from Lisa's work get smacked by the tram car."

"Bummer!"

"Yeah. We're on our way back to the motel to make sure everything's alright there. Lisa is a model employee, you see," Vinny tried to lighten the mood with a bit of humor. "Aren't you working?" Vinny asked. He turned to Rick and said, "Joey runs the rides on Sportland Pier."

"I got the night off. You're not going to be long are you?"

"Why?"

"Well," Joey said, looking enthused. "Do you remember Ernest Evans?"

Vinny scratched his chin. "Yeah! Couple of years behind us in high school, right? Used to hang around with Fabian Forte?"

"That's him!"

"Fabian!" Rick blurted, recalling that the teen idol had gone to high school with Vinny.

Vinny ignored Rick's interjection. "I remember Ernest singing and telling jokes down at some poultry stand in the Italian Market."

"Yeah, well he's still singing. He's performing over at the Rainbow Club tonight. Wanna come?"

"How about it ladies?" Vinny asked. "Once we make sure everything is squared away at the motel, why don't we show a little support for a fellow South Philadelphian?"

"Alright Joey, we'll see you there," Vinny said after the girls had assented.

"Oh my!" Joyce gasped as they started down the ramp leading from the boards to 24th Street. Up the block they could see the spinning red lights of two police cars parked at the motel.

"The plot thickens," Rick commented under his breath.

When they reached the motel, they watched one of the officers vanish into Room 11. Another policeman came storming out of the office. "Where in blazes is the manager?" he called out, throwing up his hands.

The foursome hurried over to him. "Officer, my name is Lisa Carmani. I work here. We were just on the boardwalk and saw the clerk, his name is Mel Sterling, get hit by the tram car. He was unconscious and taken away in an ambulance."

"That was the clerk from here, eh?" he asked. "I heard about the accident on the car radio," he nodded toward his prowler. "What the devil was he doing up on the boardwalk if he was supposed to be manning the desk here?" the officer asked.

"We have no idea," Rick interposed. "That's why we came back. We wanted to make sure that everything was alright."

"Well, it's a long way from alright, son. First we've got a stiff and now a clerk who vacates the premises for no apparent reason."

"Stiff?" Joyce breathed in a near whisper.

The group exchanged astonished glances.

The officer called out, "Hey Charlie! Charlie!" When the other policeman's head poked from Mr. Shapiro's door he continued, "That accident with the tram car; that was the clerk who was supposed to be here minding the desk."

"Excuse me, officer," Rick drew the talkative policeman's attention back to them. "Did you say you've got a dead body here?"

"Oh yeah. Guy in #11. Dead as Julius Caesar, that one."

"What was the cause of death?" Rick asked.

"Yet to be determined," the chatty policeman replied. "Sad state of affairs too, how the body was discovered, I mean. Some kids were playing with a beach ball in the pool and it bounced in through his open door. Kid went in after it and found the guy. Hey missy," he turned to Lisa, pulling out a notepad and pencil. "Step inside a minute. We're lucky you showed up!"

All four of the friends moved into the office while the officer extracted information from Lisa. She was able to give him the phone number of the motel's owner as well as show him the register containing Mr. Shapiro's information.

She also drew some papers from a drawer that contained Mel's employee records. The officer phoned the motel's owner and once he confirmed he was en route, the two couples were allowed to go on their way.

"Wow! What a night!" Vinny said as they climbed into the car. "Those rides were exciting enough and then the accident on the boardwalk and now a dead guy!"

Vinny parked the Bel Air on Spicer Avenue between New Jersey and Arctic. It was as close as he could get to the night club district along Pacific Avenue. After he and Rick had secured the convertible top in place, the couples walked eastward along Spicer. The streets were busy with the commotion of a summer night in Wildwood.

As they approached the corner of Spicer and Pacific, Rick could see the lights of their destination. Each side of the building's stone veneer was decorated with large letters spelling out "RAINBOW." The entrance was on the corner above which sat a curved overhang where the words "Musical Bar" glowed in neon brilliance. The side of the sign featured a marquee adorned with the name "Chubby Checker."

"Chubby Checker?" Rick mused. "Didn't he have a song out last year where he mimicked a bunch of other artists? What was it called... *The Class*?"

Vinny laughed, recalling the comical number. "Yeah, that's right."

"I thought Joey said that your classmate was playing tonight; what was his name? Ernest?"

"*That's* Ernest," Lisa said, pointing to the sign. "He adopted a stage name. Vince, didn't Dick Clark's wife give him the name?"

"The Checker part. A lot of people called him 'Chubby.' Mrs. Clark made a joke about it based off of Fats Domino and it stuck."

"I've got the first round," Rick said to Vinny after they had found a small table near the dance floor. "What'll it be?"

"We'll each take a Schmidt's," Vinny ordered for the girls as well.

"What's a Schmidt's?"

"It's a Philadelphia beer."

"Ah, another regional delicacy," Rick smiled. Soon he was back with four bottles. "Mmm," he remarked after taking a sip. "You score again, Vin. Hundredth anniversary?" he noted, looking at the small commemorative seal on the neck. He took another swig and grunted approvingly. "It's no wonder they've been around so long."

The couples munched some pretzels as they enjoyed their beer. "So what do you suppose happened to that songwriter, Mr. Shapiro?" Joyce asked.

"He died."

"Very funny, Vinny," Joyce returned. "No I mean it. Don't you think it's mysterious that he's found dead and Mel was away from the motel at the same time? Why wasn't he at the desk?"

"It certainly is bizarre," Rick added.

"You were a policeman Rick. Do you think Mr. Shapiro was murdered?" her voice dropped as she spoke the last word.

"Oh, I'd have no idea, Joyce. We'll have to wait and see. It will make the papers for sure."

Lisa cast her pretty, dark eyes on Rick. "It does seem strange though, doesn't it? That Mel was on the boardwalk rather than at the motel?"

"Yes, it does. Why don't we go and see him at the hospital tomorrow? Maybe he'll explain it himself. After all, you might've saved his life."

Lisa smiled. "That's taking it a bit far."

"Oh I don't know about that. He was bleeding pretty badly. If you hadn't taken charge and applied pressure to the wound with those towels..."

"And don't forget that she let everyone know that he had a fractured skull. What if someone roughly tried to move him? His brains might've spilled out the back of his head." Vinny added.

"Oh, here's Ernest," Joyce said, still calling the performer by the name by which she had known him.

The well-dressed, handsome eighteen-year-old stepped onto the stage. He welcomed the crowd to the Rainbow and promptly began his act.

"Hey, he's good," Rick said, nudging Vinny.

"Rick," Lisa brought her lips close to his ear to be heard above the music. "Do you think this business at the motel has anything to do with Johnny's disappearance?"

Rick shrugged. He patted her hand. "I'm going to talk to his manager tomorrow. I'll get to the bottom of it," he reassured, despite his misgivings.

"Yo guys! You made it!" Joey announced, his head appearing over Vinny's shoulder. "I see a table for two over there," he said. "We'll catch up with you later."

After a few numbers Chubby Checker announced that he was going to debut a new song for the crowd. He told them that he had a new dance that went along with it and invited them onto the floor. Two bars into the song and the whole place was up and moving to the infectious beat.

"Hey that looks like fun. Let's go!" Vinny grabbed Joyce by the hand. "Come on," he said to Rick and Lisa and they quickly followed.

The foursome joined in the great time all were having. As they mimicked the singer's moves, and listened to the lyrics, Rick stated, *"The Twist?!* This is going to catch on; you watch!"

The next morning dawned with an overcast and sullen sky. Whether it would rain or not was tough to tell, but the thick, gray blanket that hung overhead was dismal compared to the bright, sunny days that acted as the backdrop for postcards promoting the joys of the Jersey shore.

The young men sat at the breakfast table munching their toast and Corn Flakes. "Is that today's paper?" Rick asked.

"Sure," Aunt Marie said, handing it to Rick. "Just be careful with it, please. The boys upstairs like to look at it too."

Rick paged through the periodical and after a few minutes, refolded the paper and pushed it to the edge of the table.

"Anything?" asked Vinny.

"Not about Shapiro. I guess it's too soon. There's a short bit about Mel's accident. Nothing that we didn't already know, though."

They decided that they would spend the morning attending to the small lawn area that fronted the efficiency units. The friends made practical use of hedge clippers and a reel mower and some good old fashioned weed-pulling took care of the errant invaders that had despoiled the turf. After a good three hours work, the plot was ship shape.

As Vinny stepped from the kitchen door onto the driveway Rick rounded the house, returning from the tool shed.

"Aunt Marie needs me to head over to Bonelli's and get some mortadella, pancetta, and prosciutto di parma."

"Umm. Yeah. Whatever that is..."

"It's Italian lunch meat, stunad."

"Can you handle that alone or do you need me to make sure you don't wander off somewhere?" Rick returned the jibe. "Lisa set it up for me to talk to her cousin's manager."

"Yeah, sure. Go be the hero," Vinny waved his hand.

"This guy is staying in the Crest. Is it ok if I use that bike in the shed?"

"That old thing? Sure. Just make sure you don't mess with the baseball cards in the spokes. Aunt Marie likes it to sound like a motorcycle when she's popping wheelies," he joked.

After a quick shower Rick was pedaling off on his assignment. He decided to head down to the beachfront in order to enjoy the slight breeze that was blowing off of the Atlantic. Soon he was cruising southward along Ocean Avenue and found himself marveling at the ostentatious and quasi-exotic motels that lined the street. A sombrero decorated the sign of the *Siesta Motel*. He peered at the apartments behind the main building and couldn't help but be impressed at their resemblance to a Mexican village. He smiled at the plastic palm trees springing from a peninsula that extended into the unique "C" shaped pool of *The Caribbean*.

Making a right on Buttercup, he headed toward the bay. Several blocks back he found the home he was looking for. The place was a small cottage. The house was not unattractive but it was tiny and quaint, particularly in comparison to the grandiose motels that lined the beach block. Rick dismounted the bike and leaned it against one of the pillars that bracketed the porch steps. He hustled up the stairs and rapped on the screen door.

"Just a minute," an elderly man's voice echoed from somewhere within. A shuffling could be heard and then the door opened to reveal a short bald man wearing a white tank undershirt and plaid shorts. "Yes?"

He was a bit taken aback by the man's leisurely attire. "Hello, my name is Rick Walker. Lisa Carmani asked me to come over and speak with you."

"Eh? Lisa who?"

"Lisa Carmani," Rick replied, a bit befuddled by the man's confusion. "About her cousin, Johnny."

"Johnny? The singing fellow?"

"Yes... Lisa said that she told you I was coming..."

"You don't want me. You want Rudy. He's around back. Just go through that little gate there," he pointed to the side of the property.

"Oh. Oh, alright. I'm sorry. Around back, then?"

"Right through that gate," the old fellow pointed again.

Rick left the porch and passed through the chain link entranceway and followed a narrow concrete path to the rear of the house. There he found an even smaller "mother-in-law suite" that jutted perpendicularly from the rear of the cottage. He knocked on the screen door.

"Yes? Oh, you must be Lisa's friend," the man said as he opened the door. "Come in."

Rick was slow to respond however. The man standing before him was none other than the one who had stormed Dick Clark's stage at the Starlight Ballroom.

After a moment Rick recovered and stepped inside the small apartment. From a survey of the cramped quarters it was apparent that Rudy Moredello was not yet the big shot talent manager he aspired to be.

"Here, sit down," he said, dusting off the red plastic seat that accompanied a small Formica table. His host took the opposite chair. "I'm so glad that you came by. I haven't been able to get anyone to listen to me!" the portly man said, his shock of gray hair bobbing as he spoke.

"I don't know how much help I'll be, but I promised your niece Lisa I'd look into it. Why don't you tell me your story?"

"Coffee?" the manager asked, grabbing the pot from the counter of the kitchenette.

"No, thanks."

Rather than refill his own mug, the host returned the pot.

"Well young man, my story is that Johnny Taylor has disappeared! But Lisa's not my niece. She's Johnny's cousin, but I'm from the other side of the family."

Rick withdrew a small notepad and pencil from the pocket of his shorts. "Let's find a starting point. When did you and Johnny arrive in town?"

"About a week ago."

"I understand that you were trying to get Johnny booked in some of the clubs. Any luck?"

The man's face grimaced. "No, not yet. They're all booked solid already. Or that's what they're telling me."

"When is the last time you saw Johnny?"

"Three days ago. I went out for a short while and when I came back, he was gone and I haven't heard from him since."

"Where did you go?"

"Huh?"

"You said that you were out when Johnny went missing. Where did you go? What time was it?"

"Oh." He took off his dark rimmed glasses and cleaned them on his shirt. "I went to The Surf Club; over on Atlantic Avenue. I guess it was about 9 p.m."

"What were you doing there?"

The manager fidgeted in his seat. "I was listening to the music and having a drink." The inflection in his voice implied: *What do you think I would be doing there?* "Johnny couldn't come; he's too young to get in. He's only nineteen. Aren't you interested in what happened to *Johnny*?" he said, in a mild, but perturbed voice.

Rick scratched a few lines in his notebook. He looked up and smiled. "I'm just trying to be thorough, Mr. Moredello."

"Oh. Oh, of course. I'm sorry. It's just that this whole thing is unsettling."

"What time did you return?"

"About 1 a.m."

"And when you got back you noticed that Johnny was gone?"

"Yes. He sleeps right there," he said, pointing to the worn sofa. When I came in, he wasn't there."

"Where did you think he was?"

"At first I thought the bathroom. But I went to use it, and he wasn't there either."

"Do you have any idea where he might have gone?"

"None!" he ran his hand nervously through his shock of gray hair. "And no one will help me. I went to the police the next morning. They told me that Wildwood is a playground for kids his age and that he'd probably turn up shortly. I went to the newspapers and they couldn't care less that a prodigy had gone missing!"

Rick sniffed at the manager's boast of Johnny's ability. He opened his mouth to pose a question but was cut off.

"You're an investigator. Or you were in the Army. They'll listen to *you*, right? The papers? The police? You have some clout!"

Rick smirked. "I don't have any *clout*, Mr. Moredello, but if I find out anything that warrants the police or the press, I'll definitely involve them." He shifted, asking: "How did Johnny feel about trying to break into show business?"

"What do you mean?" he returned, as if Rick had made an incomprehensible query.

"Well, did he like performing? Did he want to be a singer?"

"Oh." The manager laughed. "You're barking up the wrong tree there, Mr. Walker. Johnny was made for entertaining. And yes, he loved performing."

Rick scribbled a bit on his pad. "Do Johnny's parents know that he's missing?"

"His dad died in Korea and his mother, my sister, passed away two years ago. Johnny's been staying with me ever since."

"Did Johnny have any enemies? Did he owe anyone money?"

"Owe anyone money? No. Enemies? Everyone loves Johnny. He's very charismatic. It's why he's going to be a star. He not only has a gifted voice, but he's got that 'it' factor that makes for stardom."

"How about you?"

"Eh?"

"Do you have any enemies?" He lifted his pencil point from the pad and looked into the manager's eyes.

"What? Me? Oh... you're supposing someone is trying to get to me through Johnny? No, everybody loves me too." He smiled, but the grin didn't exactly ring true.

"So in your opinion, there's no foul play involved here?"

"Foul play?" a pensive expression settled over the manager's face. "I... I don't know... I mean, I didn't think so. What kind of foul play do you think it could be?"

Rick replied, "Mr. Moredello, I didn't say that there was anything nefarious at work here but when someone goes missing it's either voluntary or involuntary. If Johnny didn't leave by choice..." Rick saw that Moredello was engrossed in thought. "I'm guessing that you asked the landlord if he noticed anything the night Johnny disappeared."

"The Chipanskis? Yes, I asked them but they said they went to bed early and as far as they knew, Johnny was still in the apartment when they retired."

"Who was Johnny hanging around with while he was in town?" Rick queried, wondering where he could next focus his attention since Rudy Moredello had not given him much to work with.

"Mostly, he stayed here and practiced, and helped me get the press stuff together," he pointed to the coffee table where stacks of papers and some 45 records sat. "But a couple of times he went down to the beach with Lisa and her friends."

"Mind if I take one of these?" Rick asked, reaching over to the coffee table and grabbing a head shot of the attractive, thin Italian boy."

"No, by all means."

87

Rick exhaled, disappointed that his inquiry had had not amounted to much. "Alright Mr. Moredello," he said, standing. "I'll be back in touch. Do you have a phone here?"

"Well no, but the Chipanski's will let me use theirs." He recited the number, which Rick scribbled in his pad. "They'll come and get me or take a message if I'm not here." Rick wrote the phone exchange for Aunt Marie's house on a separate page. He tore it from the book and handed it to the manager. "Here's the number where I'm staying."

"Okay, thanks," Rudy replied, taking the paper and placing it under a magnet on the front of the icebox.

As Rick was walking out the door, he paused and turned back. "Mr. Moredello, one last question before I leave. Why were you so determined to get at Dick Clark the night he was hosting the hop at the Starlight Ballroom?"

Photo courtesy of the Wildwood Historical Society

The Rainbow Club

Photo courtesy of the Wildwood Historical Society

89

The Caribbean Motel
Photo courtesy of the Wildwood Historical Society

Chapter 7

Rick mounted the bicycle under the same dull gray sky that had dawned over the island that morning. A few drops of rain splatted on the cream-colored sidewalk, but when he looked up to survey the clouds, all was quiet. Yet the canopy had that ominous look that promised a shower and it was as if the sprinkling that had just fallen had been a charitable warning from above that he had best get underway.

Rick took the most direct route back to the Holly Beach House, pedaling north up Pacific Avenue. He shot an occasional glance at the darkening skies but his mind was preoccupied with the explanation the manager had given him for his aggressive behavior at the Starlight. "I suppose it's plausible..." he muttered to himself.

He had barely stowed the bike in the shed when the rain came. It wasn't heavy, but the drizzle fell in a steady sheet that made the quick entry to the kitchen a welcome one. After an inspection of the bedroom and parlor, he called out for Vinny.

"Up here, on the front porch!" echoed back through the house.

"Oh, here you are," Rick said, emerging through the screen door and depositing himself in the rocker next to his friend.

"You didn't see me when you rode in? I was sitting right here."

"No," laughed Rick. "I guess my mind was elsewhere."

"How'd your big interview go?"

"Not much there. The kid went missing a few nights back when Moredello was out at one of the clubs. He doesn't know where he might've gone, or why he might've left."

"Oh well," Vinny shrugged. "Like you said, he'll probably turn up. Maybe he met a girl," the dark-haired Italian boy flashed a grin.

"You know," Rick said, seeming not to hear his friend's comments. "I saw him-- Rudy Moredello-- trying to push his way up to Dick Clark that night at the Starlight. The bouncers tossed him."

"Huh? Really? I didn't see that."

"You were off getting a Coke."

"You didn't say anything about it."

"I had no idea who he was until I met him today. I asked him about it and he said that he had considered that the best way to locate Johnny would be to get the word out amongst his peers. With hundreds of teens at the dance he wanted Dick Clark to make an announcement to see if anyone had seen the singer or if not, to be on the lookout and give contact information should they see him. But unfortunately the security men at the ballroom had taken his actions as a disruption and would not even listen to him, even after they escorted him from the stage."

Vinny nodded but when his friend stayed quiet he added, "So?"

"I don't know Vin. I guess if he was really worried it might make sense but the kid was only missing a day at that point."

Vinny scratched his head. "Yeah, I suppose. But if he hadn't heard from him at all and had no idea what happened to him... He might've been worried enough to give it a try. It might have been a good idea."

Rick's head bobbed slowly as he worked over the notion. "Dick Clark seemed pretty glad to see him tossed from the stage."

"Yeah, well he *was* trying to put on a show."

"I wish I could ask Dick Clark about it."

They sat in silence for a moment and then Vinny snapped his fingers. "Follow me," he ordered and headed through the screen door. "Hey Aunt Marie," he said, finding the woman in the laundry room. "Don't you know the lady who owns the place where Dick Clark boards when he comes to Wildwood?"

"That television dance show fella, right? Oh sure, he stays at the Knoll's Motel over on Roberts and Atlantic."

"But you know the owner, right?"

"Oh sure," she repeated the phrase as she dashed some detergent into the open-tub washer. "Agnes Knoll. We play cards together."

"Do you think she could help us get in touch with him? Rick is looking into a missing person's case and has a question or two for him."

"A missing person's case?"

"Yeah, a kid went missing and his uncle is looking for him. Rick was in the Military Police when we were in the army and said that he'd help out," Vinny gave her a very abridged explanation.

"Oh, that's nice of you," she patted Rick's arm. "I'll phone Agnes. When I'm done the laundry? Okay?"

"Oh, I forgot to tell you," Vinny turned to Rick. "The girls called. They want a ride over to see Mel at the hospital. We've got to go pick them up. You might want to get situated," he said as he mussed Rick's hair, still damp from the rain. "You don't want Lisa to think you're a slob."

Ten minutes later the friends emerged from their room with combed hair and smelling of cologne. As they passed through the kitchen, Aunt Marie stopped them. "Agnes was out, but she'll phone me when she gets back. Here," she said, handing them a pair of umbrellas. "Bring them back, Vincenzo," she wagged her finger at her great-nephew.

Wibbage's DJ had aptly chosen to spin Buddy Holly's *Raining in My Heart.* The pitter-patter on the convertible's canvas top sounded a disjointed cadence as it headed up Atlantic Avenue, providing a rhythmic accompaniment to the tune wafting from the Bel Air's speakers.

"We've got to grab the girls at work," Vinny said, sensing his friend's confusion that they were headed north rather than south toward Joyce's grandmother's place on Leaming Avenue.

Vinny brought the Chevy to a stop at the corner of Atlantic and Pine in front of a red brick building. A large crimson vertical sign that hung out over the sidewalk read: "Uncle Lou's" in yellow letters. Joyce was standing under the shelter of one of the red and white striped awnings that accompanied each of the restaurant's windows. Rick jumped from the passenger seat and climbed into the back as the girl in the waitress uniform dashed to take his place.

"Busy eh?" Vinny commented as she closed the door. "The rain?"

Joyce replied, "Oh, it's actually slowing down now. Breakfast is always the busiest time. That's why they let me work just the mornings. My shift starts really early but it's over in time for me to get to the beach!"

"Not today!" Vinny said, pulling from the curb.

"No, the beach wouldn't be much fun today," she pouted as the wipers sloshed the water on the glass in front of her.

After another few minutes they had retrieved Lisa from the 24th Street Motel.

"Does Mel know we're on our way?" Vinny asked the petite girl in the chambermaid outfit.

"I called to see how he was doing but they wouldn't tell me anything. I asked to speak with him and they said he couldn't receive calls. My boss said that his parents have been notified and are on their way down. He's from Connecticut or Rhode Island or someplace."

The Bel Air headed up New Jersey Avenue, through North Wildwood. As they passed the huge, odd structure of Zaberer's restaurant, Rick's inquiries about the curious, unusual building required a short dissertation from Vinny on Ed Zaberer and the "Host of the Coast's" signature restaurant.

As they reached the end of the island, the narrow road became supported by pilings and crossbeams that reminded Rick of a railroad trestle. The pavement hovered above wetlands before reaching a drawbridge where a white sign with black lettering announced that they were about to cross an expanse of water known as "Grassy Sound."

After leaving the barrier isle, the Chevy headed westward. Rickety plank boardwalks ran out from either side of the roadway to provide access to cottages perched atop pilings in the salt marsh.

"Where is this hospital?" Rick posed.

"It's up the parkway a few miles. There used to be one on the island years back but they built a bigger facility, more centrally located so as to serve the whole county," Lisa informed.

"Makes sense," Rick returned.

Vinny pulled into the parking lot of Burdette Tomlin Memorial Hospital and promptly found a space for the Bel Air. The rain had not diminished and they were thankful for Aunt Marie's thoughtfulness in providing the umbrellas.

"May I help you?" a kindly looking elderly lady inquired as they stepped up to the front desk.

"Yes," Lisa spoke for the group. "We're here to visit Mel Sterling. I'm not sure of the room number."

"Let me see," the woman placed the glasses hanging from a cord around her neck onto the end of her nose as she consulted a ledger. "Yes. He is in 221. The elevator is over there. Stop at the nursing station when you get up there and they will take care of you."

"Thank you."

After a quick jaunt in the lift the quartet repeated their inquiry of the nurse on duty.

"You can go in briefly if you'd like, but I'm afraid that he is in a medically induced coma."

"Oh my," Joyce gasped. "Really? Will he be alright?"

"We're hopeful but it's far too early to tell."

"Excuse me," Lisa interjected. "Who is the attending physician?"

"Dr. Roth."

"I was the one who administered first aid at the scene," Lisa informed. "Before he lost consciousness, he asked which doctor would be treating him. His family is on their way down. You might want to share that with them. Maybe they have a family doctor they want consulted."

The nurse made a note. "Room 221 is right down there, around that corner," she pointed with the pen she held in her hand. "Just keep the visit under ten minutes."

As they walked down the hall, in a low voice Vinny muttered, "Well we're not going to find out why he left the motel-- unless he talks in his sleep."

"Why is he in a medically induced coma?" Joyce asked.

Lisa replied, "Sometimes with a brain injury doctors will use drugs to slow the metabolic rate of brain tissue as well as the flow of blood to the brain. This causes the blood vessels to narrow, reducing brain swelling."

Rick pushed open the door to find a room with two beds. The one closest to the door was occupied by a sleeping man who appeared to be in his mid-fifties. The other one held the unconscious form of Mel Sterling, his head wrapped in a thick white bandage. Beyond Mel a large man in a dark suit whirled toward them, his face twisting his flat nose into a startled expression.

"Oh, eh. I'm lookin' for my friend.... I think I have the wrong room."

"What's his name? Your friend?" Lisa asked. Lifting the clipboard at the foot of Mel's bed she began paging through the sheets to see if it included a patient register.

"Eh... Dick. Dick Wilson," the man grumbled.

"Is this him," Vinny sarcastically remarked, shooting his thumb toward the older man in the first bed.

"Na. Sorry. I think that nurse sent me in the wrong direction. Excuse me," he commented, pushing past the friends and exiting the room.

"He's not listed here," Lisa informed, but the man was already through the door. Mel's chart was included however, and the nursing student examined the pages with

97

great interest. Joyce and Vinny looked over her shoulder, and began asking Lisa questions about Mel's condition.

A troubled expression clouded Rick's face, unrelated to the unfortunate desk clerk. He moved across the room to the small table where the "lost" man had been standing. Rick opened the drawers as well as a small closet door next to the table. There he found the patient's clothes hanging, although his top shirt was missing, presumably ruined by the blood from the head wound.

"I'll be right back," he commented to his friends and left the room. "Excuse me," Rick announced his presence to the nurse at the station. "Do you have a patient named Dick Wilson on this floor?"

The woman didn't even have to scan her documents, demonstrating her familiarity with her patients. "No. No one by that name is in this ward."

Rick's heart beat faster. "There was a man in our friend's room when we went in. Big fella. Flat nose. Gray fedora hat."

Confusion marked her face. "There shouldn't have been."

Rick was lost in thought as they drove back to Wildwood.

"So the nurse didn't even see that guy leave?" Vinny asked.

"Eh? No. But she said he could've slipped by when she was doing some filing on the other side of the nursing station."

"And he was obviously lying about who he was there to visit too. Weird! I wonder what he was doing in the room."

"That's a good question, Vin. Attempting a robbery, maybe? Perhaps he was looking for Mel's watch in that drawer or his wallet or something. Could be he was hitting every room he could, seeing what he could find."

"How crummy!" Joyce interjected. "Trying to steal from the sick!"

"If that's what he was about, I'm sure he came away empty," Lisa responded. "Patients' wallets, watches, jewelry... anything of value gets catalogued and locked up."

"Hey, didn't you say you wanted to get souvenirs for some of your family?" Vinny asked his friend.

"What's that? Oh. Yeah."

"Well today is as good a day as any, what with the rain and all," Vinny said. "I know just the place!" He swung the car off of the Parkway at exit 6, and headed back down the long causeway that entered North Wildwood.

A short way past the gigantic Zaberer's Restaurant, Vinny slowed the car as they cruised by a long, white, one story building. Rick read "Shell Shop" above two of the many large picture windows that faced the main road. The driver made a right hand turn on North Delaware Avenue, pulling into the parking lot behind the store. The crushed clam shells that substituted for gravel crackled under the Bel Air's tires as Vinny found a space amongst the three cars already occupying the lot.

"Do you think we need the umbrellas?" Joyce asked.

"Na," Vinny replied, climbing out into the balmy mist that had replaced the rain.

"This is one of the coolest places, isn't it, Joyce?"

"Oh, yeah. I haven't been here yet this year but I always make sure I stop at least once each summer."

Rick was intrigued. He followed the procession as they walked alongside the thick rope strung from piling to piling that acted as a fence for the parking area.

A bell tinkled as Vinny pulled open the glass door at the corner of North Delaware and Spruce Avenues.

"Hello," the middle aged woman at the cash register welcomed as they stepped inside.

Rick returned the greeting as his eyes adjusted to the interior. The shop consisted of one large rectangular room. In the center was a long island separated into two dozen or so bins. More bins and shelves lined the outside walls. The net effect of this orientation was to create an oval setting where a shopper could begin at one point and examine the wares as they made their way around the room and finally back to their starting point.

If the layout was considered novel, it was nothing compared to the merchandise that occupied the space. The store was a monument to all things nautical. In fact, even items that one would not have thought to associate with the seashore had been crafted into maritime themed products.

A large brass old time diver's helmet rested alongside an upright anchor fashioned into a lamp. A ceramic lighthouse resided near a miniaturized facsimile of a pirate's chest. A stack of captain's hats took up some shelf space beside a wall clock made to resemble a starfish. A piece of wood cut to look like a sperm whale featured dowels to hold coats. A barrel held dozens of plastic pirate cutlasses... The list of oddities went on and on. A great many of the bins were devoted to holding a vast variety of exotic seashells and a handful of enthralled children were each judiciously sifting through these in order to fill the quota of "six for a quarter."

"Wow," Rick said after digesting what he saw. However his wonder reached no one's ears as the girls and Vinny had already begun perusing the interesting and curious stock.

"What 'cha got there?" Vinny asked.

"Oh, I'm grabbing some of these shells for my nieces... And I got this crab, see?" Rick winded a small key on the back of the red tin toy. He put it down on the shelf and the thing made a sideways scurry across the surface.

"Look here," Vinny said, showing Rick a post card.

"Ahhh, the Golden Nugget. Is that for Georgie?"

"Yup. He'll be eating his heart out to get down here and ride it," Vinny winked mischievously.

"Hey. I think I'll get this for myself."

"A telescope? Why would you want that?" Vinny asked.

"Oh I don't know. Maybe on the beach I can get a better look at a sailboat. Or maybe if some dolphins come along..." He collapsed the spyglass and added it to his basket.

"Oh that's nice," Joyce said, looking over Lisa's shoulder at the water color painting she held.

"Hereford Lighthouse," Rick read, joining them. "Where is that?"

"It's here in North Wildwood. Hereford Inlet is the area between North Wildwood and Stone Harbor."

The friends spent a solid hour in the Shell Shop, each glad that Vinny had made the suggestion. Like so many who entered the store, Rick vowed to make it a regular stop should he be fortunate enough to spend other vacations on the island.

After dropping the girls at Joyce's grandmother's house, they headed back to the Burk Avenue.

"Hey, look here. There's a piece on Shapiro," Rick said, grabbing a newspaper from the sofa as he sat down.

"Oh yeah? Does it say how he died? Was he murdered?" Vinny asked, depositing himself in the chair adjacent to the couch.

Rick was silent as he scanned the article. "The autopsy is pending but there was no evidence of trauma."

"In English, sport."

"His head wasn't bashed in. His throat wasn't cut. He wasn't strangled. It looks like natural causes but until they run a toxicology report-- that's a fancy word for poison-- they can't be sure that he expired on his own."

"Thanks, professor."

"So, your aunt called the woman who owns the Knoll Motel and asked about contacting Dick Clark?"

"Yeah, she talked to her. Mrs. Knoll said she'd see what she could do," Vinny shrugged. "We'll see." He got up and peered out the window at the misty rain that continued to fall. "How about some Gin Rummy?

"Sure," Rick folded the newspaper and tossed it onto the coffee table.

As the afternoon wore on, the dismal weather continued but that gloom was mitigated by the wonderful aroma wafting from the kitchen. Aunt Marie could be heard bustling about, singing some melody in the language of her ancestors. The shrill bell of the telephone broke into the Italian aria and a moment later she was calling for Rick.

"Me?" he asked rhetorically at the unexpected summons. Vinny leaned to one side to see the television screen as Rick passed in front of it as Tony Gonzalez had just made contact with a Don Drysdale fastball.

"Hello?" he asked, after lifting the avocado green handset sitting atop the wall-mounted telephone.

"Hello, is this Rick?

"Yes; speaking."

"This is Dick Clark."

"Oh," Rick's voice lifted in a surprised tone. "Mr. Clark. Thanks for calling."

"Mrs. Knoll said that you were investigating a missing person's case? How can I be of help?"

"Well, the person in question is a local singer named Johnny Taylor. I was at your show at the Starlight Ballroom the other night and I noticed that Johnny's manager, Rudy Moredello, made an unsuccessful attempt to reach you on stage. I was wondering what that was all about."

"That fellow has been hounding me to no end." The famous DJ laughed. "At first in Philadelphia and then down in Wildwood. Weeks ago he cornered me and forced his nephew's record on me. I even listened to it. But... there's nothing special there. At least not in that recording. But he won't let up. He keeps badgering me to play the record." He chortled, "He even told me that I should put his nephew on Bandstand! On national television..." he laughed and Rick could almost see him shaking his head. "...without even a single station playing his record."

"He's been hounding you quite a bit, huh?"

"To put it mildly."

"Hmm. Well that certainly explains why you barred him from the stage."

"You say that his nephew is missing?" Dick Clark interjected, as if he had just made the connection.

"Yes, Mr. Moredello said that he was trying to get to you on stage to ask you to announce that Johnny had gone missing and tell the kids to be on the lookout."

"I wonder if that's true... I mean that he wasn't going to try to get me to spin his record," the voice on the other end of the line contemplated. "Have you uncovered anything?"

"He's only been gone a few days and I'm trying to figure out if there's anything amiss or if he just went off on his own."

"His uncle is overbearing," Clark commented. "I wouldn't be surprised if the kid needed some breathing room. I'm sorry to cut you short, but I've really got to be going. Is there anything else I can help you with?"

"No. Thank you, Mr. Clark. I was just trying to clarify what was going on that night at the Starlight. You've been very helpful. Thank you for calling."

"No problem. Take care. Moredello is a pain but I certainly hope that Johnny is okay. Bye now."

"Who was that? Lisa?" Vinny asked as Rick returned to his seat on the sofa.

"Dick Clark..." he replied in a subdued tone as he rubbed his chin in thought.

The name jarred Vinny from his ballgame. "Dick Clark?" He smirked. "I guess Aunt Marie came through. What'd he have to say?"

"He said that Rudy Moredello had been pestering him to boost Johnny's career. He wanted Clark to play his records on Bandstand or even give him a live performance."

"So when he showed up at the Starlight trying to get on stage, Dick Clark just figured it was more of the same and didn't want him interrupting the show," Vinny postulated.

"Hey Vin, what can you tell me about Rudy?"

"Moredello? Not much."

Rick chuckled. "That's a first; it seemed like all of the Italians from South Philadelphia are intertwined."

"I know he's from Philly, but he's not from my neighborhood. I could call my pop and see if he's got any dope."

"Could you? I think I need to know a little more about Johnny's manager."

Grassy Sound Bridge

Photo courtesy of the Wildwood Historical Society

The Shell Shop

Photo courtesy of the Wildwood Historical Society

Chapter 8

"Alright, they want to go."

"What's playing?"

"A Doris Day picture," Vinny replied, grabbing a hanger and removing the clean shirt it held.

"Did you phone your dad?"

"Yeah. He's going to ask around about Rudy. He'll call back once he has something to report."

Vinny clicked the switch on the little radio that sat on the table between the beds and the dial glowed to life. "Hey, don't tell me I don't treat you right," Hy Lit's voice entered the room. "That was *Love Is A Many Splendored Thing* by the Four Aces. Now I'll turn it over to that dear friend of mine, Mr. Sam Cooke."

Vinny grabbed the hairbrush from the dresser and began to serenade his friend with a lip-synced rendition of *You Send Me*. He moved around the room as he "sang" mimicking the facial expressions and hand gesticulations of one giving the performance of their life.

"Come on, you goof!" Rick pulled a wet towel from the bedpost and hurled it at his pal. The cloth landed atop Vinny's head, making him appear like an Arab sheik, but he continued his recital nonetheless.

Rick pushed his way past his friend and splashed some aftershave into his palm. Rubbing his hands together, he then lightly slapped at his face like a drowsy person trying to wake himself up. But he was fully alert, and eager for another date with the pretty girl with the flashing black eyes.

The murky weather had dissolved with the sunset, leaving a crisp, clean aroma in the night air. Stars had begun to twinkle to life as the last pink-lemonade hues faded in the western sky.

The tires of the Bel Air hummed warmly on the grating of the George Redding Bridge as it headed away from the barrier island. The Coasters' *Yakety Yak* emanating from the car radio echoed off of the concrete embankments and overhead steel girders as they cruised under the Garden State Parkway overpass at Exit 4. When the Chevy cleared the Parkway, the large illuminated sign of the Wildwood Drive-In Theatre loomed off to the right. The placard read: "Doris Day in *Please Don't Eat the Daisies* also *Pillow Talk*."

After settling up at the entrance booth, Vinny brought the Bel Air along the gravel path that led to the open field facing the huge projection screen. The unpaved ground was ringed with rows of curved berms that radiated out from the giant screen like the ripples of a pebble dropped in a pond. He found a suitable spot toward the rear and eased the car up to the pole that protruded from the ground. The front of the Chevy crept up the berm, creating a comfortable angle for viewing the show. The young man cranked his window up a few inches and removed the box speaker from its harness atop the pole, carefully hanging it on the window.

"So, what'll it be? Popcorn? Hotdogs? Shrimp rolls?" Vinny asked, rubbing his hands together.

"Oh, popcorn would be fine. Maybe something to drink," the girls announced after conferring.

"Alright, we'll be right back."

The procession of headlights filing into the outdoor theater had begun to thin as show time approached. The friends joined the growing crowd funneling toward the concession stand, ready to stock up before the miracle of motion pictures transformed the massive white rectangle into an instrument of entertainment.

Nightfall had fully descended and as the two pals stood in line, they witnessed the warming glow of the beam shoot from the small porthole of the projection blockhouse. Suddenly the nearest speaker crackled to life. A brief stanza of parade music accompanied an image on the screen suggesting that patrons visit the "Snack Center." A jovial voice announced that the show would start in eight minutes. A mock circus took its place on the screen as a cartoon cup danced, juggling popcorn with a pair of stringy arms. This performer was soon joined by a frankfurter turning several summersaults before landing in a bun. Candy bars walked a high wire and soft drinks twirled straws as if they were batons. The countdown continued as the announcer warned that the show would begin in seven minutes.

As Rick waited to be served, he thought back to the call they had received just before leaving the house. Vinny's dad had come through with some information regarding Rudy Moredello. According Mr. Valenti's sources the man was not in debt, and no one seemed to hold any ill will toward him. The would-be talent mogul was in actuality the proprietor of a small television repair shop. The shop did alright but Rudy Moredello aspired to far greater things and could often be found inflating his accomplishments. From all accounts the man was competent and worked hard, but apparently believed that in order to become a bigwig, he had to prematurely portray himself as one.

"Two big buckets of popcorn," Vinny said as he stepped up to the window. "And four orange drinks."

The concession girl asked, "When you say 'big buckets of popcorn,' do you mean large, extra large, or jumbo?"

"Huh? The big one," Vinny pointed over her shoulder to the containers displayed atop the popcorn machine.

She turned to where the cartons were stacked and grabbed a pair of the second smallest in the lot.

"Hey! No! The big one!" he pointed again to the display.

"This *is* the big one," she said over her shoulder. With a look of consternation she stated, "We have big," she shook the cup she had in her hand. "Big means large." She pointed to the next size up, this is extra large or as some would say *bigger*. Finally we have jumbo, or the *biggest*."

"That one!" The irritated Italian boy pointed emphatically. "You can call it atom bomb size for all I care but I want two of those!"

The girl shrugged and began to fill two of the proper containers.

"Unbelievable!" Vinny rolled his eyes.

"I hope we don't have to go through the same business with the drinks," Rick whispered to his buddy.

By the time Rick and Vinny were back at the car, the antics of the animated foodstuffs had ended and the announcer gave a gentle reminder to replace the speaker on the post after the show. This brought a chuckle to Rick's lips as he realized the warning must have its foundation in reality. He imagined someone attempting to roll up their window upon reaching home only to realize they had driven off with the thing still in place.

The couples enjoyed the feature film, laughing at the interplay between Doris Day and David Niven. The antics of the New York couple, their four boys and oversized sheep

109

dog trying to adjust to life in a rundown country mansion made for ample entertainment.

"Joyce," Lisa called from the back seat as the credits rolled. "I'm going to make a trip to the ladies' room."

"I'm coming," her friend replied.

"Hey girls," Vinny said, delaying their departure. "You've both seen this next one, *Pillow Talk*, right?" he asked of the upcoming picture that was in fact a second run film having come out the previous year.

"Yes, Vincent. I told you that already," Joyce chided.

"Alright, just making sure."

When the girls' returned, the top was up on the convertible.

"What gives?" Joyce asked.

"Well…" Vinny replied with a twinkle in his eye. "Since we've all seen this flick, we figured maybe we could do with a little bit of privacy, should, you know, it get chilly and it become necessary to warm you girls up."

The girls smiled at each other but made no protest. Nothing that was to go on in the Bel Air that night was any coarser then what occurred on screen between Rock Hudson and Doris Day. However when the film ended that couple's affection dissolved into nothingness but the two young men and their dates were becoming even more enamored with one another.

The next morning brought a cloudless day. After breakfast the friends spent their time sanding the spindles along the front porch. It was tiring work and by the time they called it quits they still hadn't made it to the second floor of the double-decker structure.

"How about tomorrow we paint these rather than sanding the ones on the top porch," Rick said, pointing toward the spindles. "And then we sand the top ones after that."

"Yeah, Okay," Vinny wiped his sweating brow with his forearm. "Might as well. The place looks like a haunted house with these unpainted. Let's get this stuff put away and hit the showers."

The couple from Unit 1 passed by decked out for the beach. "Hard at work, eh?" the middle-aged man said as he toted a folding chair past the duo.

"Just finishing up," Rick returned.

"You've got the right idea, just working in the morning. I think it's going to be a hot one today. So long," he waved as he and his wife turned from the driveway and headed up Burk Avenue.

As they showered they could hear the family from Unit 2 similarly heading out for their day at the beach. The youngster's cap pistols blazed away as the patriarch tried to coax the boy into helping drag the make-shift beach wagon.

Within the hour Rick and Vinny were on their way to the beach themselves, again making the trek to Hand Avenue. Despite the crowd, it didn't take long before they found the blankets of their gang.

"Yo Vin!" Joey called out the greeting as he adjusted the radio, tuning in The Platters *The Great Pretender*.

"Where are the girls?"

"What do you think *we* are?" Connie asked, dropping her sunglasses to the tip of her nose.

"Yeah Vin," Connie's friend Angela added. "Not for nothin' but these are bikinis we're wearing you know."

"Yeah I guess you two qualify," Vinny smirked. "Even though Angie was in my shop class."

111

"Hey! You know that that was a mistake. That goofy counselor messed up my schedule!"

Mike chimed in, "You mean where are *your* girls. Don't fret Casanova, I'm sure they'll be along shortly. Hey, look what I brought," Mike held up a broomstick with one end wrapped in electrical tape.

"What are we going to do with that?" Vinny asked.

"What do you think, genius?"

"Um, hey Einstein, we can't play stickball on the beach. How are you going to bounce the ball? You've got to bounce it to pitch. And don't tell me down there on the hard sand. There are tons of people down there. Somebody'd get clobbered."

Mike tossed a strangely shaped object which Vinny snagged out of the air. Rick peered curiously at the item. It was a white "pimple ball" but there was something missing… half of the ball!

"Ah, a game of half-ball eh?" Vinny said. "But how are we going to play without a building? "You see," Vinny turned to Rick. "With half-ball you use a building as a backdrop. If you hit the wall on the first floor in the air, that's a single, second floor a double, third a triple. On the roof is a homer. If anyone catches it off of the building, it doesn't matter where it hit, it's an out."

Mike interjected to answer Vinny's question. "Well we've improvised games on our street our whole lives, Vin. I was thinking that we put markers on the sand out from home plate and just use distance rather than height to determine single, double, etcetera, etcetera."

"Could work," Vinny rubbed his chin. "Alright, let's shoot for first at bat! Odds or evens?"

The makeshift game commenced. Rick had never even imagined that someone might try to hit half of a ball. This game was totally foreign to him and the South Philly kids were extremely adept at not only hitting, but pitching as well. It was apparent that a lot of time had been spent perfecting methods of making the half-ball curve, rise, and dive. Yet Rick was athletically inclined and before long he was getting the hang of it. Just as the game ended Joyce and Lisa arrived on the scene.

"Oh, I'm glad you're here," Lisa said in a serious voice as she pulled Rick off to one side.

"I'm happy to see you too," he joked.

"Listen," she said, "Irving Shapiro's daughter came down to the motel today to collect his things."

"Really?" Rick's interest perked up.

"Get this. She said that her dad was in Wildwood to do some work. That he loved to relax down the shore while he was writing. She said that she had spoken to him the day he died and he had said that he'd just put the finishing touches on a masterpiece!"

"Like a symphony?" Rick said it straight-faced but Lisa knew he was joking, and slapped him on the arm.

"No, dummy. A pop tune. But a sure hit. She said that he had written so many, he never seemed excited about a song, but this time he was. But guess what? No song was found in his room! His daughter wants to know where the song is!"

Rick scratched at his temple. "Do you think whoever cleaned the room might've thrown it away?"

Lisa shook her head. "*I* cleaned the room!"

"Hmm. Well this thing keeps getting more interesting, doesn't it? Mel leaves the motel for some unknown reason and a successful songwriter turns up dead on the premises, presumably from natural causes-- if the papers have it right. And now a song he was writing has also disappeared." Rick

113

was silent for a full thirty seconds. "Any word on Mel's condition?"

"They still have him in the induced coma."

"Well, breaking our brains on this beautiful day isn't going to help any. How about a dip?"

The girl's black eyes crinkled into a smile. "Alright. Race you!" With that she took off toward the Atlantic.

After half an hour in the ocean, the couple returned to the blanket and enjoyed their lunch.

"Philadelphia, Daily News!" a boy cried out in a sing-songy voice. "Philadelphia, Daily News!"

Vinny threw his hand into the air. "Over here!" He turned to Joey. "The Phils are still on the west coast. I wonder how they made out last night." As he plopped a coin in the kid's palm, the boy pulled a folded newspaper from the bag slung over his shoulder. "Ahh! Lost again!" Vinny blurted, but continued to read on to get the details.

Joey rolled up his beach towel and got to his feet. "See ya. I gotta go. I'm running the Hell Hole tonight."

"The *what*?" Rick asked.

Joey laughed. "Remember, I work up on Sportland Pier. It's one of the rides."

"Oh, it's awful," Joyce said to Rick. "It's this circular room. You go in and it spins. It spins so fast that the centrifugal force pins you to the wall. Then the floor drops out!" She shuddered. "I've only been on it once and the guy next to me puked! It plastered to the wall right between us!"

"Oh!" Rick returned. "I was on a ride like that once at an amusement park. They called it the *Gravitron*. I know exactly what you're talking about."

"See you later," Joey waved as he headed off.

Just then Lisa tapped Rick on the arm. "Look at that!"

The drone of the sign plane hadn't even registered with him. He had become accustomed to the sound his first day on the beach as several dozen had buzzed along, advertising the restaurants, clubs, and attractions of the Wildwoods. However, when he followed Lisa's pointing finger, what he saw brought him to full attention. The banner trailing the plane read: *Want To See Johnny Taylor Again?*

Vinny came jogging over to them. "What do you suppose that is all about?" he asked.

"I don't know..." Rick mused. "But I aim to find out."

"Mr. Chipanski?" He spoke into the handset. "Mr. Chipanski, may I speak with Mr. Moredello? This is Rick Walker... Oh. Oh, I see. Do you know...? Oh, okay. Well, will you please tell him I phoned? In fact, have him call me. The number is..." He consulted the paper tag under the plastic center of the dialing mechanism and read the telephone exchange to Johnny Taylor's landlord just in case Rudy had lost the copy he'd affixed to his refrigerator. "Alright. Thank you. Bye."

"No dice, huh?" Vinny asked as he pulled a pitcher of lemonade from the Kelvinator icebox and filled two glasses.

"No," Rick returned, accepting the drink his friend handed to him. "He's out and the landlord doesn't know where he went or when he'll return." He brought the glass up to his lips but dropped it back down without taking a sip. "Hand me that phone book, will you?" he pointed toward the thick yellow volume on the small shelf just to his friend's right.

Vinny leaned back and retrieved the object. "Here you go." He downed some lemonade and then came around behind his friend. "Ahh, looking for the banner plane outfit, eh?"

"Yeah. I'm guessing they can tell me who paid for that sign."

Rick found the number and moved over to the telephone. After the dial had spun around the final time, a voice came through the earpiece. "Paramount Air Service."

"Hello, I'm trying to find out some information on a banner I saw flying over the Wildwood beach today."

"Hmm. Well I just answer the phones. You would have to speak with the owner, Mr. Tomalino but he's out on the field right now. We've still got a few flights to make. Can I have him call you back?"

"You're at the county airport, right?" Rick asked, looking down at the advertisement in the telephone directory.

"Yup."

"How far is that from Wildwood?"

"Oh, ten minutes, tops."

"I think maybe I'll take a drive out. Thanks." Rick replaced the round earpiece in the chrome "Y" of the cradle. "Feel like taking a ride out to the county airport?"

The duration of the trip was no longer than the employee of Paramount Air Service had promised and it was easy to zero in on the banner plane operation once they had arrived at the airport. In the distance they heard the unmistakable, characteristic drone of one of the sturdy, reliable, Piper Cubs used by the business.
Vinny braked the car to a halt. Through the windshield they spied one of the sign planes descending from the far end of

the field. The pilot brought his craft over the runway, although it became apparent that he had no intention of landing. The friends watched the aircraft with great interest, wondering what the pilot had in mind. As the plane passed, the long banner it was towing released and fluttered to the ground. Two boys scurried from a nearby building and retrieved the sign.

After discarding the banner the pilot had begun guiding the plane in a long arch, indicating that he was circling back to the runway. When the plane neared the airfield again its wings tilted to and fro as the flyer maneuvered the airplane so that it was in line with two poles about six feet apart and surprisingly, only about four or five feet high. The Piper Cub dropped down at what looked to be a forty-five degree angle as it zoomed toward the poles. When it reached the spot, a bar dangling from the bottom of the fuselage neatly hooked a line strung between the poles. Suddenly the pilot pulled back on the stick and the plane shot into a steep climb. As it headed upward and outward, slack was taken up and a new sign that had been lying on the field began following the banner plane as it buzzed off toward the beach.

"Pretty neat set up," Vinny said, stepping from the car.

"I'll say. Efficient, too. The pilot doesn't even have to land to change banners."

As the friends approached the building a handsome middle aged man stepped into view, his aviator sunglasses reflecting the late afternoon sunlight. He turned toward the two boys who had snatched the discarded banner. "That was the last one," he pointed after the retreating plane. "He'll make one pass over the Wildwoods and drop it, and then you can call it a day."

"Hi there," Rick said as he approached.

117

"Hi."

Rick extended his hand. "My name's Rick Walker and this is my pal Vince Valenti."

"Andre Tomalino. What can I do for you?"

"I've got to tell you, I never imagined that that was the way these planes picked up the banners," Rick laughed. "I just assumed they had to land and take off with them attached."

"That's how they did it back in the 20s and 30s. I was a glider pilot in the war. I came up with this system, modeled on how our tow planes handled the gliders."

"Army Air Corps, huh? We were in the army too," Rick said. "I was an M.P. One of our friends asked me to look into a missing persons case, which is what brought me out here to see you."

"To see me? How can I help?" the sign plane innovator asked.

"The missing person is a young man named Johnny Taylor. Today we saw a banner plane fly by that said *Want to See Johnny Taylor Again?* I was hoping you could tell me who commissioned that sign."

The Air Corps vet scratched his head. "I'd like to help you, but I doubt that I can." The man laughed sardonically. "We got that order by mail. There was no signature, just instructions to fly it over the Wildwoods."

"Let me guess," Rick said. "They didn't pay by check."

"Right. There was cash in the envelope along with the message. Enough for one pass over the island." He took off his sunglasses and cleaned the lenses on his shirt. "*Now* that message seems cryptic," he pondered. "I just assumed that he was a performer, you know, a singer or comic at one of the clubs and the point was to get patrons to come back to see another show."

"Didn't you find it odd the way the request came? I mean, paid in cash, with no identification as to the customer?"

"You'd be surprised," he chuckled. "Established businesses usually handle things in a more orderly fashion but a lot of private people hire our planes. I've gotten wedding proposals written on the back of napkins, birth announcements on cash register receipts." He shrugged.

"When did you receive it?"

"Yesterday."

"Would you happen to still have the note?"

"No, it got tossed."

"How about the envelope?"

"No that went out with the trash too."

"Would it be too much to ask to go through your trash? Maybe I could find it."

"We've got an oil drum out back where we burn that stuff. It was fired up this morning. Sorry," the banner plane proprietor said.

Rick rubbed the back of his neck with his palm. "I don't suppose you would happen to have looked at the postmark."

"No," the aviator shook his head. "I'm sorry. I really wish that I could help you."

Rick pulled out his notepad and dragged his pencil across a sheet. "If you do come upon anything you think might be of interest, please give me a call," he said, handing the page to the banner plane proprietor.

WILDWOOD
DRIVE-IN THEATRE

RIO GRANDE — PHONE 2-7418

DELSEA DRIVE - RT. 47

Exit 4A, Garden State Parkway
BOX OFFICE OPENS 7:30
SHOW STARTS 8:35 P. M.
CHILDREN UNDER 12 YEARS FREE

Thurs., Fri., Sat., May 22-23-24
Lana Turner - Lee Philips
Hope Lang - Lloyd Nolan in

"PEYTON PLACE"

An absorbing story of a Town, Its
People, It's Moments of Sadness
and Gladness.
In CinemaScope and Color
PLUS
Diana Dors and Rod Steiger in

"THE UNHOLY WIFE"

Half Angel - Half She Devil, She
made him half a man.
COME EARLY
ONLY 1 COMPLETE SHOWING

Sun., Mon., Tues., May 25-26-27
Rita Hayworth - Jack Lemmon
Robert Mitchum in

"FIRE DOWN BELOW"

The most shameless she in The
Carabee, scorching the heart of
every man that knew her.
In CinemaScope and Color
And Randolph Scott
And Maureen O'Sullivan in

"THE TALL T"

A mile high in courage, adventure,
entertainment.

Photos courtesy of the Wildwood Historical Society

120

Chapter 9

"You sure you don't want to come along?" Rick asked as his friend tuned in the Phillies game on the television.

"Na, you two kids have fun. If Joyce didn't take that dinner shift for her friend, we'd have come with you but I don't want to be a third wheel."

"Hey, we don't mind, we're only going to take a walk up on the boardwalk and grab a light dinner."

"Don't sweat it," Vinny waved his hand. "I'll be happy watching the Phils."

Vinny didn't feel he had the right to loan Rick his uncle's car but had offered to drive the couple down toward the piers, and pick them up when they phoned. However it was a cool, pleasant night so he and Lisa decided that they would enjoy making the whole trip on foot. They planned on strolling the boards, unsure if they would even venture onto the amusement piers.

Rick pulled on a light windbreaker and walked south to Joyce's grandmother's house on Leaming Avenue. From there the pair headed east, straight up to the boardwalk where they joined the multitudes of vacationers crowding the famous pathway.

"So, nothing yet on Johnny?" Lisa's voice was strong but Rick could detect a hint of uneasiness, as if she had practiced the line to mask her angst.

He grabbed her hand and patted it reassuringly. "Not yet. But remember what I told you. There's no indication of anything shady. If something dreadful had happened to him, he would've showed up in the hospital or..." he thought better of finishing that thought. "Anyway, like I said before, he probably met a nice girl or maybe needed a break from Rudy. That's what Dick Clark suggested, anyway."

Rick's words did reassure the young co-ed but the slight smile that creased her lips was also partly from the fact that he had neglected to release her hand. As she sauntered over the boards her fingers interlaced with the handsome young man, more seemed right in the world than wrong.

"Are you getting hungry?"

"A little," the petite girl replied.

"What shall we have? I've heard a lot about pizza on the boardwalk. How does that sound?"

"Oh, that'd be great. Let's go to Mack's. There's one right up there at Robert's Avenue."

Rick could see the blinking sign for the pizza parlor two blocks away. "Mack's... yeah I remember seeing the name when we were up here before but I thought it was further on."

"You're not wrong; they have four restaurants on the boardwalk. It's great pizza. Wait until you try it; and this coming from an Italian from South Philly!"

The couple seated themselves at the counter next to two adolescent boys. The kids were sharing a pie with their parents who sat on the stools to their right.

"What can I get you?" A dark haired man in a white shirt asked.

"Well Lisa, you're the local. You tell the man," Rick said.

"We'll have two slices and two birch beers."

The man nodded. "There will be a fresh pie coming out of the oven in a minute." While he waited on the pizza pie, the man went over to a large brown barrel that sat upright on the corner of the counter. A sign affixed to it pictured the profile of an Amish fellow and words that read: *Pennsylvania Dutch Birch Beer*. The counterman grabbed hold of the handle of the tap protruding from the side of the barrel and filled first one cup and then another.

"I've had root beer," Rick said, a reflective look in his eyes, "but I don't think I've ever had birch beer before."

"It's similar, but I think it's better."

Rick took a sip. He found it difficult to differentiate the drink from root beer. Perhaps a tad bit sweeter, he thought. "Ha, look at that," he said pointing toward the island counter in front of the pizza ovens. "Now that's a clever idea!" At the work station a white-shirted man was using a hose to apply tomato sauce to the pie he was making.

"I think they invented that," Lisa said.

"Pretty neat. I guess they have a giant stash of the sauce in the basement or something," Rick speculated, his eyes following the hose as it disappeared down into the counter. "I never saw that either," he said, pointing toward the pie the man was creating. "Putting the cheese on first, and then the tomato sauce next."

"Here you go," the server had returned, dropping two napkins before the couple, a slice atop each paper square.

Rick read the wooden sign on the wall stating that a slice was 29 cents and a drink 15. He placed a dollar atop the counter and the man rung up the purchase and slid his change back across the linoleum.

"Looks good," Rick said of the thin slice, the oil from the cheese glistening under the florescent lights. After one bite the young man had a new favorite food.

"Excuse us," the father of the boys next to them said as he and his family slid past them and back out onto the boardwalk.

"Oh, no trouble," Lisa returned.

"Would you like another?" Rick asked Lisa after he had devoured his own slice.

She smiled, as she was not even done the one she had in hand. "No, this will be plenty. Thanks."

"Excuse me," he called to the dark-haired fellow. "Can I get another slice?" As the man went to fill his order, Rick had to promise himself that he would stop there, for he truly believed that he could eat an entire pie on his own.

As the couple got up to leave, Rick spied a pouch on the counter where the boys had been. "What's this?" He picked it up and slackened the drawstring. Peering inside he said, "Marbles."

Lisa chuckled. "They must be in the tournament."

"Tournament?"

"The National Marbles Tournament. Wildwood used to host it but the past ten years or so it's been held other places. This year its back and city officials have said that they plan on keeping it here as a tradition."

"Well, I don't know much about marbles but maybe that kid is partial to using his own. I'll hold onto these," he said, shoving the pouch into the pocket of his windbreaker. "Maybe we'll see them on the boardwalk and I can return them." He pulled out his pad and scratched a quick notation. "Excuse me," he called to the counterman. "I found a bag of marbles. If anybody comes looking for them, here's the phone number where I'm staying."

As odd as it may sound, despite the multitudes of people; the flashing lights, and buzzers and bells of the games of chance, it was really the first time they had had any solitude. Prior to this they had always been with Vinny and Joyce or their whole gang. The couple meandered northward along the boardwalk, enjoying each other's company.

"I know we just ate, but man does that smell good," Rick said, breathing in the scent of roasted peanuts. He stopped to look up at the extravagant blinking lights of the store in front of them. Yellow bulbs trimmed in red neon spelled out: NUT HUT. The rendition of a small house sat between the two words, an avalanche of peanuts spilling from its door. Below this sign another lighted advertisement read: "Fresh Roasted Nuts- Whipped Cream- Fudge- Salt Water Taffy."

"That reminds me. I promised my mom to send back some fudge from Laura's," Lisa commented.

"They have fudge here," he pointed to the sign.

"Oh, my mom is very particular. Laura's is just off the boardwalk on Wildwood Avenue. They have this vanilla walnut fudge to die for. Try to remind me to stop."

As they walked on, he read a sign above a shop and posed another question: "What's a *Lime Ricky*?"

Lisa laughed. "It's sort of like a cross between an Italian ice and limeade. It's sweet and a bit sour at the same time. It's kind of hard to describe."

"That sounds interesting," Rick pulled her toward the shop but as they neared the storefront, he suddenly froze in his tracks.

Through the cluttered noise of the boardwalk Rick overheard someone near him scornfully say, "I'm telling you, Johnny Taylor is a ham."

"You're dead wrong. Follow me, I'll show you," came an indignant reply. A bell from a nearby game rang shrilly, obscuring most of the next sentence, but the fellow ended with, "dork!"

"What is it?" Lisa asked, alarmed at Rick's abrupt halt.

125

He put his finger to his lips. Leading her by the hand he pulled her off to trail the retreating men. After their quarry was a good distance ahead he informed Lisa of what he had overheard. "It was only a couple of sentences but the one seems to dislike Johnny, implying he's a show off. The other one said that he's wrong, called him a dork, and said to follow him and he'd prove that he was wrong."

"How do you know they were talking about my cousin?"

"He said Johnny Taylor."

"Those two, there?" she pointed toward a pair of young men in their early twenties.

"Uh huh. That's them."

"So you think they know where Johnny is?" she asked excitedly.

Rick answered without taking his eyes from the pair they were surreptitiously following down the boardwalk. "The one ordered his buddy to follow him and he'd demonstrate that he was wrong about Johnny. He knows something; that's for sure."

They navigated through the swarm of people as they tailed the two young men. A child's balloon obscured Rick's view and he side-stepped to see around the obstacle.

They continued their surveillance, carefully shadowing the pair. Rick wondered how the fellow had been able to come to the conclusion that Johnny was a prima donna. It didn't seem that the singer would have had the opportunity for people to critique him. From what he knew, Johnny had had very few public performances. Perhaps the man had heard the promo record, as Dick Clark had... But could one be considered a "ham" merely from the sound of his voice? It didn't seem possible. "No," he thought. "To label someone a show off, they would have had to witness a performance."

The yellow train of the tram car approached from the other direction, creating a barrier between Rick and Lisa and the pair they were trailing. The lead car, sporting the blue insignia of *Sightseer* braked to a halt to pick up a fare. The couple continued their pace as Rick peered through the open cars attempting to keep his eyes on their targets. His gaze circumvented the smiling faces of dozens of riders whose buoyant expressions and jovial laughter contrasted greatly with the seriousness that he had assumed in his role as a shadow.

Lisa's face likewise revealed a conversion in her demeanor. Moments before she had been playfully enjoying her night out with the handsome young man from Ohio but now a hopeful earnestness, an anxious anticipation, had overtaken her visage.

As the pursuit dragged on Rick tried to speculate on where they were headed. However, try as he might he could not fathom where the man could be dragging his companion to show him that he was wrong about Johnny Taylor.

Suddenly the pair they were tailing halted. The man who had led the way pointed upward. The other man shook his head and also pointed in the same direction. Rick longed to hear what they were saying. He decided that he must act.

"Come on," Rick said, tugging Lisa ahead. Quickly, they closed the gap and were at the side of the arguing duo. "Hey," Rick said, addressing the two bluntly. "Do you know where Johnny Taylor is?"

The pair stopped dead in their disagreement and both looked at the intruder with furrowed brows.

"Answer me. Do you know where Johnny Taylor is?"

Lisa's pretty mouth opened expectantly, her heart pounding in her chest.

"Who?" the one he had overheard criticizing Johnny replied.

"Don't play dumb," Rick asserted. "Johnny Taylor. The singer. I heard you call him a ham."

The man gave Rick a quizzical look and a moment later burst out laughing. His friend soon joined him in his fit.

Rick and Lisa exchanged confused expressions.

"Listen pal," the young man said, recovering from his mirth. "I don't know any Johnny Taylor. I was trying to convince my friend here; *Johnny*, that taylor is ham. You know, like the sandwich." He pointed up at the sign of the eatery in front of them. Dark green lettering on a rectangular white sign read: TAYLOR PORK ROLL Sandwiches.

Rick's jaw dropped as he read the marquee.

"I'm from North Jersey," the man continued. "My buddy here is from down this way and insists that it's not called "taylor ham" but a "pork roll."

A crimson hue glowed over Rick's face. "I'm sorry," he muttered patting the man on the arm. The embarrassed investigator trudged over to one of the benches that border the beach side of the boardwalk. He pulled the hinged back so that it faced out toward the ocean and dejectedly flopped onto the seat. His pretty companion took the place next to him.

"I'm a little confused," Lisa finally said.

Rick exhaled. "It's my fault. I misread the whole thing. When that guy said to his friend, *I'm telling you, Johnny Taylor is a ham.* I must've psychologically misplaced the comma; your cousin's disappearance being on my mind. He must've really said, *I'm telling you Johnny, taylor is a ham."* His friend returned that he was 'dead wrong' and said *follow me, I'll show you.* I couldn't make out some of his next sentence but I thought it ended with him calling his friend a 'dork.' Now I know better. That last word was *pork."*

Lisa sighed heavily. Although it had only been a few minutes that her hopes had been lifted, the unhappy conclusion of their little chase still stung.

"I'm sorry, Lisa," Rick shook his head, irritated with himself. "I shouldn't have even told you what I thought I overheard. I should have just told you to wait for me while I went and confronted them."

"Oh, don't be crazy. You wanted to follow them, not confront them and it would've been pretty hard to convince me to stay put while you ran off. By the time you gave me an explanation I would've accepted, they would've been lost in the crowd."

"I guess. Still I wish I didn't tell you. Not only did I give you false hope by jumping the gun, I made myself out to look like a real goof." He kicked at the metal rail that ran along the edge of the boardwalk. "I should've been more professional. I just got worked up when I thought that clue fell in my lap."

The two sat quietly for a moment. "Taylor ham versus pork roll," she muttered. "...the age old argument." Despite the sad reality that her cousin was still missing, the pretty girl began to chuckle.

Rick looked over at the smiling dark eyes and had to crack a grin himself. He joined her in a good laugh. "I have to admit," he said, "I've been outfoxed before, but this is the first time that I was beaten by a sandwich."

"Hey, you know what? I've got just the place to lighten the mood. Come on," Lisa said, taking him by the hand.

"Where are we going?"

"This way," she said as they re-entered the multitudes carousing on the boardwalk. Lisa led the way to the block between Schellenger and Lincoln Avenues. "You'll get a kick out of this place," Lisa said, stopping in front of a red, white, and blue awning.

Rick looked up at the sign that extended out over the boardwalk. The face of a clown was pictured next to the words *Fun Shop*. He peered at the glass window cases that bracketed the doorway, observing the multitude of gimmicks and gags on display. He smiled at Lisa. "This is going to be good," he said and entered the store.

The place was busy. Children and adults alike crowded the shop. Near the entrance a boy brought his hand down on the counter, expelling the air from a whoopee cushion. He and a companion roared with laughter at the flatulent sound effect.

"Here, try some," a clerk said, handing a teenage boy a stick of gum. The young man's eyes narrowed and his nose crinkled as he slid the stick into his mouth.

Apparently he had been anticipating an unsavory flavor, saying to the girl next to him, "Hey, it doesn't taste bad." However, when she began to laugh, he realized that he had not escaped unscathed. She pulled a compact from her purse, revealing to him that his lips had turned pitch black.

Rick and Lisa moved over to the counter on the right side of the shop, examining a great variety of masks, wigs and eyeglasses.

"How do I look?" Lisa asked, affixing a fake moustache under her nose.

Rick shook his head. "You won't be getting any kisses from me with that thing." Much to his delight she quickly removed the item as if his threat was a powerful motivator.

An enthused kid wearing a red cowboy hat tapped Lisa on the arm. "Watch this," he said, digging into a small box filled with saw dust. His thumb and forefinger emerged holding a tiny piece of twisted white tissue paper. The boy threw the object at the floor as hard as he could. Immediately there was a "snap" sound. "Pretty cool, huh? Man, are the boys back home going to dig this!" he beamed.

"Care for some fake dog poop?" Rick asked, pointing the item out to Lisa.

"Hmm," she rubbed her chin thoughtfully. "My parents did just get a new carpet. I suppose it might be fun to watch my dad throw a fit," she smiled. "No..." she reconsidered. "He might end up killing the dog before I was able to clue him in on the prank."

"I like this one," Rick said, lifting a catsup squeeze bottle from the counter. He pointed it at Lisa and tightened his grip, causing a red string to shoot from the bottle. To the unsuspecting picnicker, the gag would certainly trigger a moment of fear.

There was a lot to see in the store and just navigating the crowd to get a peek at all of the displays was challenging. Still, both considered it time well spent as they laughed and joked about dozens of the gag gifts.

A magic section existed toward the back of the shop where one of the employees was entertaining a group by performing card tricks.

"How did he do that?" Lisa asked after a patron had chosen a card and ripped it up as instructed, only to have it emerge whole again from inside the performer's top hat.

Rick shrugged. "If you really want to know, I'll buy you the set he's selling," he smiled.

"No, that's okay. The last way I want to spend my time is practicing card tricks."

For a few minutes Lisa lost track of Rick but he appeared again with a small bag in his hand.

"What's that?"

"Oh," he smiled. "Just a present for Vinny," he winked without revealing the contents. He tucked the bag into the inside pocket of his windbreaker.

The couple spent nearly forty-five minutes in the Fun Shop, and the visit had indeed lifted their spirits after what they would later jokingly call "the pork roll misadventure."

"Laura's Fudge!" Rick said, snapping his fingers as they exited the Fun Shop. "I was supposed to remind you."

"Good job," her black eyes sparkled up at him. "Let's go take care of that now."

They headed three blocks north to Wildwood Avenue and crossed over to the ramp. Before they had even descended to the street, their destination grandly revealed itself. At the junction with Ocean Avenue stood a large pink building, its signage a dazzling combination of flashing bulbs and glowing neon. "Laura's" appeared over the angled door and the name of the establishment was bracketed along both Ocean and Wildwood Avenues with the lighted word "Fudge" as two pixie-like characters happily stirred tubs of the treat.

The interior was painted in a festive pink and white scheme and like so many renowned businesses on the island, the candy store was busy. It took a few minutes before they were able to approach the counter but the cheerful young lady who waited on them was quickly able to provide Lisa with the vanilla walnut fudge she desired. Learning that Rick had never even heard of the variety

132

before, the salesgirl provided a sample. Rick was so taken with the taste that he purchased a small quantity to bring back to the Holly Beach House.

The couple ambled back up to the boardwalk and headed south once again. They stopped to get a frozen custard and by the time they were nearing the end of the boardwalk at Cresse Avenue, the last of Lisa's cone had disappeared between her thin lips.

"What say we head out onto the beach?" Rick asked, looking toward the flecks of moonlight reflected from the sea.

Lisa nodded a reply and led him to sit down on the steps where they removed their shoes. The sand was cool as they walked out toward the sound of the whispering surf. Rick helped the petite girl up onto the lifeguard stand and hauled himself up next to her. The soothing noise of the waves, the refreshing salt air, the stars twinkling on the dark horizon and the company of a very special young man... Over the years, even at oddly random times, that summer night would come back to Lisa and it never failed to bring a smile to her lips.

Photo courtesy of Anne Vinci

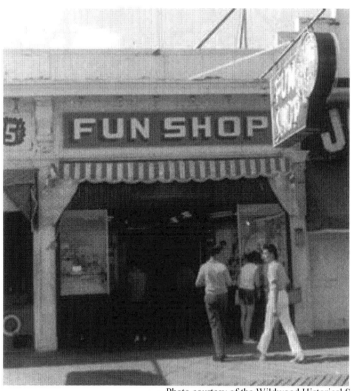

Photo courtesy of the Wildwood Historical Society

Laura's Fudge

Photo courtesy of the Wildwood Historical Society

Chapter 10

Rick and Vinny awoke to a bright, clear day. After breakfast they tackled the upper level of the porch, sanding and painting the spindles that lined the railing. They also replaced a few of the floorboards that were in poor shape.

It took a bit of scrubbing to clean themselves up after their morning of work, and even then a number of their friends on the beach pointed out places on their arms and legs still marked with tan paint.

The beach that day was every bit as wonderful as their previous excursions. The ocean was warm and the breakers were just rough enough for the body surfing Rick had come to relish. The sky was nearly cloudless for the entire afternoon, the powder blue brilliance interrupted only by the white streaks of contrails as the state of the art Boeing 707s and Douglas DC-8s ferried passengers up and down the east coast. Truth be told, there was one distraction from the fun. Every time the drone of a Piper Cub sounded, Rick, Lisa and Vinny waited in secretive anticipation until the banner could be read. However, none of the planes towed another message about the missing singer.

"Mr. Chipanski," Rick said into the mouthpiece. "What do you mean Rudy can't come to the phone? Alright, alright. When you see him tell him to call me. Good bye."

"What's up?" Vinny asked, pulling a few grapes from the bowl on the kitchen table and popping them into his mouth.

"Ahh!" he waved his hand in aggravation. "That Rudy Mordello is in the apartment but he's not answering. The landlord isn't too happy about having to stand there banging on his door." Rick ran his hand through his brown hair. "I'm going over there," he said with deliberation. "I need to find out if he was behind that sign plane message the other day."

"Want me to come along?"

"Na. Why don't you check the papers and see if there's anything you and the girls would like to do tonight. On the beach I heard someone say that Buddy Hackett is appearing at the Bolero."

"Alright, that's a good idea. I'll see what's going on and then give the girls a call and get their opinion."

Rick disappeared into the bedroom for a minute. His intuition was telling him that his interaction with Rudy Moredello might require some action that was less than straight forward. He shoved a cylindrical object into his pocket before leaving the Holly Beach House.

He opted not to take the bicycle down to Rudy's apartment in the Crest. Rick wanted to mull over the case before he got to his destination and pedaling along the busy streets would require his senses to be on the alert. Rudy's place was on West Buttercup, so Rick made a right on Burk Avenue when he left Aunt Marie's. He then headed south along Pacific Avenue. As he walked, he turned the events over in his mind.

Rick passed through the gate at the Chipanski's cottage and trod up to the door of the mother-in-law suite. He rapped on the wood. Leaning forward, he heard movement inside. He knocked again. The door opened and Rudy Moredello's gray head appeared in the opening.

"Oh, Rick Walker. Do you have news?" he asked anxiously, without inviting his visitor inside.

Rick ignored the question. "Did you commission a banner plane to advertise Johnny's disappearance?"

"What?" Rudy's shock was palpable.

"So you didn't hire a banner plane to pull a sign reading: *Want to See Johnny Taylor Again?*"

"What... What are you talking about?" he stammered.

"Just what I said," Rick stated flatly. "Yesterday on the beach a plane flew by towing the banner I just described."

Rudy Moredello began to fidget nervously. His eyes darted back and forth. "No. I didn't hire that plane. I... I have to go. I have a meeting." He went to close the door, but suddenly his demeanor changed, and he opened it again and stepped outside. "This may be important," he said, trying to mask his anxiousness. "Please, follow up with it and let me know what you find out."

"I'll do that," Rick replied without revealing his trip to Paramount Air Service. Something was amiss and he decided that Rudy should not be privy to full disclosure.

"Ok. I really do have to go. Thank you for coming by, though," Rudy reiterated, before stepping back inside.

Rick left the backyard and pushed through the chain-link gate. However, rather than heading back toward the Holly Beach House, he circled the block, stopping at a three story building on Lavender Road. The dwelling's backyard butted against those on Buttercup but was two houses east of the Chipanski's cottage. The place had a shed behind it and Rick crept down the driveway and behind the shed. From this spot he could see the apartment of Rudy Moredello.

Reaching into his pocket, he produced the telescope he had bought at the Shell Shop. Rick extended the device and crouching down, rested the spyglass on the top rail of the chain-link fence that separated the backyards of the two properties. He could see Rudy moving about inside of the apartment. His actions were hurried, as he travelled from the living room to the bedroom and back again. Suddenly the door flew open and Johnny's manager exited and stormed off at a hasty pace. At the gate he made a right, heading toward Pacific Avenue.

Rick acted quickly. He left his vantage point and at a quick clip hustled eastward to the corner of Lavender and Pacific. Suddenly however, his heart skipped a beat. Rudy had turned south on Pacific and was headed in his direction. Rick quickly retreated fifty feet and ducked behind a two-tone green Nash station wagon. He breathed a sigh of relief when Moredello crossed Pacific and headed eastward on Lavender. The watcher crossed the street and followed at a considerable distance, using the parked cars to screen him.

Rudy walked with a brisk, determined stride. He advanced in the direction of the ocean but once he passed Atlantic Avenue he stopped, heading under the canopy of the Aztec Motel.

Rick crept up the opposite side of Lavender Road until he was adjacent to the motel, which he curiously found to sport a southwestern desert theme rather than any motif featuring the ancient civilization for which it was named.

Peering through the windows of a powder-blue Plymouth Fury he spied his subject inside a telephone booth. The investigator pulled out his telescope. He watched Rudy dial a number, speak briefly and then hang up. The man stayed in the booth, however. A moment later the shrill ring of the phone could be heard and Rudy quickly scooped the handset from its cradle. Through his spyglass he was able to make out the contorted features on Rudy's face. "He's unhappy about something, that's for sure," Rick said to himself. The disgruntled manager's free hand jerked up and down as he punctuated his animated conversation.

After a few minutes Moredello angrily slammed the receiver home and pushed open the bi-folding door of the phone booth. He ran his hand through the shock of gray hair atop his head and began to pace the sidewalk next to the Aztec. Back and forth he went, seeming to talk to himself as he wore a groove in the pavement.

Rick shoved the spyglass into his pocket and crossed the street with deliberation. "Rudy!" he called out, aggravation causing him to lose the more respectful address of "Mr. Moredello." The startled man looked up. An expression of fearful alarm passed over his face and for a moment it appeared as if he were about to run. He took a step but seemed to think better of attempting to outdistance the athletic young man now not thirty feet from him.

"Rudy," Rick repeated after he had reached the man. "I've had enough of this. Its time you came clean."

The portly man's shoulders shook in a disingenuous laugh as his eyes crinkled behind the lenses of his dark rimmed glasses. "What are you talking about? I think you're imagining things."

"Excuse me," Rick said, pushing past him into the open telephone booth. He began fishing through his pocket for a coin.

"What are you doing?" Rudy nervously asked.

"I'm calling the police. That's what you wanted before, right? You wanted the police involved but they wouldn't pay any attention to you? Well now you're going to get your wish. I'm guessing however that your attitude may

140

have changed since then." He hesitated before dropping the dime into the slot and looked over at the panicky manager.

"Alright. Alright. Let's talk," Rudy replied as he gratefully watched Rick shove the coin back into his pocket. "Not here on the street. Let's go get a cup of coffee. Follow me." With that the defeated man trudged off toward Atlantic Avenue.

In silence the pair walked southward on Atlantic. Rick thought better of trying to discuss the situation before they reached the restaurant. He strode with a confident air, his back stiff and his chin high. While a member of the Military Police many times he had escorted a prisoner in a similar way and he wanted to convey the same image to Rudy Moredello-- that he had been ensnared. That he had been beaten and was being shepherded to be interrogated.

Despite the seriousness of the situation, Rick couldn't help but be momentarily distracted by the large motel that lay ahead. The building had a space-age look to it, enhanced by the blue neon letters inscribed on its sign reading *Satellite*. The word was highlighted by yellow stars and *Motel* was spelled out in red neon across the bottom.

However their destination was not the motel but the similarly designed eatery right next to it, Shumann's Restaurant. The broad, pitched roofline gave the place its own futuristic look. Rudy turned and walked under the extended brown awning that stretched all the way to the street.

The interior was cavernous, a great room with cylindrical lights hanging from the exposed beams. The staff was beginning to ready the place for the dinner crowd and a few early bird patrons had already taken spots at the yellow tabled booths.

"Two?" the hostess asked, beginning to lead them toward a booth.

"Uh, we're just going to have some coffee," Rick interjected. "The counter will be fine. Thanks." The girl smiled and returned the two menus she had grabbed. The counter was unoccupied but Rick led Rudy to the farthest of the teal colored stools nonetheless.

"What can I get you?" an attentive woman with a beehive hair-do asked.

"Two coffees, please," Rick ordered.

In a matter of a minute a pair of steaming mugs sat in front of them. The waitress had retreated, leaving them alone in their corner of the restaurant.

"So, let's have it," Rick commanded.

Rudy sighed heavily. He tilted the glass sugar container, sending a stream of white crystals through its chrome top and into the brown liquid. Dropping a spoon into the beverage he began to sullenly stir. "I don't know what I'm going to do," he groaned.

"You were behind it; the disappearance. It was your idea," Rick said, giving voice to an idea he had tucked into the back of his mind but had only confirmed by Rudy's recent shady behavior.

The gray head nodded.

"I'm guessing that it was a publicity stunt, meant to get Johnny some attention?"

"Yeah. But nobody cared. I couldn't get anyone to pay any notice."

"So when the papers wouldn't listen and Dick Clark wouldn't give you any publicity, you hoped that I might stir some interest. That's why you jumped at Lisa's suggestion that I get involved."

"Uh huh, but nobody cared about you either," he said, almost mockingly.

Rick took a sip from his coffee. "So... you obviously didn't commission the sign plane. Who did?"

Rudy began to fidget in his seat. "I... You see, I needed help to pull off the disappearance. Some guys I know in Philly... Well they put me in contact with this fella, Sal. I offered him a deal. I told him the plan, and I said I'd give him a ten percent stake in Johnny's career once it took off. Since the plan wasn't working I gave up on it. I just wanted Johnny to show up again and say that he'd run off with some dame for awhile. But Sal... Well it turns out Sal tried that banner plane stunt to see if it would jump start the plan." He nervously took a sip from his coffee cup. "It didn't work, obviously."

"So where is Johnny?"

Rudy gulped. "I don't know."

"You don't know?" Rick said incredulously

"You see, I had to insulate myself." Rudy's voice had a pleading tone to it. "That's why I brought in Sal. He's got a criminal record. If things went bad, I thought that he would be afraid he'd take the fall. I could deny any involvement and I thought he'd split-- take a powder."

Rick had brought the coffee to his lips but put the mug back on the counter before taking a sip. "So let me get this straight. You knowingly let some thug abduct your nephew and keep you in the dark as much as possible to protect yourself."

Rudy's chin dropped to his chest. "I... I was trying to do what was best for Johnny. For his career." His tone was so pathetic it didn't even seem as if he believed his own lips.

"Did this guy Sal rough Johnny up— to kidnap him? I mean if you were trying to insulate yourself, I'm guessing that Johnny doesn't know you were involved."

Rudy suddenly looked up as if the thought had never occurred to him. "No. No, I had him tell Johnny that we were setting up a record deal. That him vanishing briefly was the idea of the record company, in order to build anticipation. I've even spoken to him a few times. He seems fine."

"I'm guessing that if things went sour your plan was to tell Johnny that Sal forced you to play along, threatening to harm Johnny if you didn't."

Rudy nodded.

"So, the jig is up. The grand scheme didn't work. Why are you so distraught? Johnny comes back to you and you do your best to build his career the legit way. Nobody really noticed he was gone except Lisa and you could just feed her your line about Johnny running off with a girl for awhile."

"Yeah. The thing is that Sal now wants me to give him $5,000 to release Johnny."

Rick shook his head. "Oh what a tangled web we weave... So when I told you about the banner plane, you knew that if you didn't hire it, it had to be Sal. You rushed off to contact him, to ask him what he was up to and he told you that it was his last ditch effort to get your plan to work. Since it didn't spur any more interest in Johnny's disappearance, he went to his own plan: blackmailing you, using Johnny as collateral."

"He says I conned him. He says that I guaranteed that the plan would work and Johnny's career would take off. He says he's owed the five grand." Rudy grimaced. "I don't have five grand!" he nearly exclaimed in exasperation, catching himself mid sentence and lowering his voice again.

Rick sat silent for a moment. "How does Irving Shapiro factor into this?"

Rudy sat bolt upright at the mention of the dead songwriter and a panicked expression crossed his face. Almost instantaneously his features changed to a calm, nonchalant appearance. "Who?" he asked, un-convincingly.

"No more games, Rudy. Let me guess. You told Sal that Shapiro was in town and said that if Johnny could record the song he was writing, it would ensure that Johnny would have a hit."

Rudy nodded grimly. "Sal said that he could persuade Shapiro to let Johnny record the song."

"And in true Moredello fashion, you again tried to insulate yourself. You didn't want to know *how* Sal would *persuade* him."

"He... He didn't kill him. The papers said that Shapiro died of natural causes."

"Perhaps," Rick retorted with a grunt, disgusted by the actions of the man next to him. "The music he was working on wasn't found in the room. So if Sal stole it, why not just release Johnny and have him record the song?"

"Sal didn't steal the song. He said that some kid working at the motel took it."

It was Rick's turn to be shocked. He turned to Rudy. "Sal is a big guy, with a flat nose. Wears a gray fedora," he said, describing the man they had found in Mel's hospital room.

Rudy nodded again. "That's him. How did you know?"

"Let's just say I know the type." He took another swig of his coffee. "Well Rudy, I suppose it's time we went to the police."

"What? We can't do that!"

"I don't see what else *can* be done." Rick shrugged. "You don't have the $5,000."

"But... But he might hurt Johnny!"

Rick was unsure if Rudy's concern for Johnny's health outweighed his worry over implicating himself if they went to the police. "You know Rudy," he said, swiveling his stool to face the man. "If you play around with a rattlesnake, you might get bitten. *You* brought this Sal character into this knowing that he was a crook. You thought you were so smart that you'd protect yourself by enlisting the help of a convicted felon. Think about what I just said: *Protect yourself by enlisting the help of a convicted felon.* How stupid does that sound? Yet that was your brainstorm."

Rudy's hands were shaking. "He... he really might hurt him, you know. If he found out that I went to the cops..." His body quaked in a shudder of distress that seemed genuine.

"In the phone booth you had to call a number and then wait for Sal to ring you up, so I'm guessing that you don't even know his phone number. Someone had to tell him to call you back, is that right?"

He nodded solemnly. "All part of trying to insulate myself," he mumbled.

Rick spun his stool back toward the counter. He pushed his fingertip into some coffee that had spilled on the linoleum and traced several circles for a long moment. "Alright," he said, looking again at Rudy. "I have an idea. But if it falls through, there's no other choice-- we'll have to go to the police."

Photos courtesy of the Wildwood Historical Society

Chapter 11

The crowd was thinner then on his previous trips to the boardwalk, but it was still busy. The hour was getting late and the population was decidedly different from his earlier experiences. Gone were the youngsters bouncing wildly, tugging their parents toward the whirling lights and chaotic motion of the amusement piers. He crossed paths with a few zonked out tykes slumped in their strollers who's exhaustion was so complete that they showed incredible immunity to the noisy disharmonic sounds all about them. However, by and large those left treading the famed walkway were in their late teens or young adults.

Rick made a beeline for the Fun Shop and once inside, approached an area where he and Lisa had enjoyed a few laughs. The wigs, glasses, false teeth and other items all seemed absurdly funny at the time but at present some of the things sold here would be helpful in a task that was far from humorous.

He selected a pair of tortoise shell rimmed glasses and carefully picked through an assortment of false mustaches until he found one that matched the brown of his hair.

"Can I see that mirror?"

"Ha! You look like a new man," the clerk said, handing him the looking glass.

"That's the idea," he muttered under his breath as he examined his new appearance.

After paying for the items he made a further stop in a store that sold beach accessories. There he outfitted himself with one of the stingy brim straw fedoras he saw so many vacationers wearing.

Glancing at his watch, Rick hurried northward along the boardwalk. Even at this late hour the business at the pizza place was brisk. He ordered a slice and a lemonade and took a seat at the counter. It was warm inside the restaurant and he unzipped his windbreaker. He looked at his watch again. Taking the smallest of bites from the slice, he attempted to make the piece of pizza last as long as possible. Again he tilted his wrist. The minute hand had moved almost ten places. He began to fidget in his seat.

Rick picked up a brochure from the counter and began to page through it, trying to extend his stay. The pamphlet advertised a tour boat called the *Sightseer*. The front tri-fold featured a big blue and white craft with signage that read: Sightseer Wildwood Cruiser. Inside, the advertisement explained that the ship was located at Ottens Harbor on the bayside of the island, only a couple of streets north of the Holly Beach House. The description of the ship's cruise along the beachfront, through the inland waterway and Cape May Canal and the wildlife it promised, would have held his attention more thoroughly if he were not so preoccupied.

Another peek at his watch and an unpleasant thought entered his mind. What if Rudy Moredello had skipped out? He was after all a self-centered and reckless man. He bolted, Rick decided. He had found himself boxed into a corner by his deceitful ploy and he had taken off. He was not going to show up at the pizza parlor.

Rick determined that he would go straight to the police station. He took a last bite of pizza and swig of lemonade and stood to leave. Suddenly he dropped back onto his stool. Rudy Moredello had just walked in. The manager seated himself at a booth facing toward Rick, as he had been instructed. Not thirty seconds elapsed before the familiar flat-nosed face of Sal appeared and the large man took the seat opposite Rudy. The waitress seemed disappointed when each only ordered a coffee, but she brought the beverages quickly nonetheless.

Rick had taken the precaution of having Rudy face his way so that Sal would be looking in the other direction. The thug had only seen him briefly in Mel's hospital room, and he was satisfied with his disguise. Still, he thought it prudent to take the extra measure of not allowing the hired goon an opportunity to stare his way.

The pair were not close enough for Rick to overhear their conversation but if Rudy was following instructions, he knew what was being said. He could see the pleading expression on Moredello's face. He appeared completely sincere in imploring the gangster to give him time to try to raise the ransom. The conversation lasted less than ten minutes. Sal stood, casually dropping his fedora upon his head. He poked a meaty finger into Rudy's chest and then condescendingly patted him on the shoulder before sauntering out onto the boardwalk.

Rick scurried from his spot ignoring Rudy Moredello as he passed, not daring to remove his eyes from the blackmailer for even a moment. He lingered at the entrance to the pizza shop long enough to give Sal a head start and then fell in behind him.

The hoodlum lumbered northward on the boardwalk. When he stopped to buy a bag of roasted peanuts, Rick slowed and moved over to a shooting gallery, feigning interest as a few young men attempted to eradicate the red star on the paper some twenty-five yards away. Sal moved off again, at the same leisurely pace, dipping his big mitt into the bag every so often.

150

Rick kept his distance as the large man continued northward. He was approaching Sportland Pier, where the shrieks of the late night patrons could be heard as the cars zoomed along the peaks and valleys of a monorail rollercoaster. The metal struts of the Ferris wheel turned slowly, looking like a blown up version of a child's erector set project.

The entrance to the Sportland Pool sat directly across from the amusement pier. Rick knew from speaking with the kids on the beach that behind the large building that acted as a gateway existed a giant pool open to the public. However the waters would be quiet now as the place closed each day at five o'clock.

At 23rd Street Sal left the boardwalk. Rick lifted his shoe to the bottom rail of the fence next to the ramp. He re-tied the lace, even though it did not need it, peering off after the retreating man. A minute later he was back in pursuit, leaving the boards himself. Two and a half blocks back, Sal made a left, disappearing from view.

Rick approached the area with caution. He crossed the street in order to examine the spot as prudently as possible. The house was a small, one story bungalow set back from the street. No light showed through the drawn shades of the enclosed front porch. Rick moved further up the street. From this vantage point he could see two yellow rectangles glowing near the rear of the bungalow.

Rick crossed and slid along the side of the house. When he reached one of the illuminated windows he slowly and carefully peeked over the sill. Through the dirty gray wire screen he could see that the room was the kitchen. Inside Sal's huge frame was seated at the table, his back to the window, the gray fedora resting upon the table. Rick's heart dropped. Sal was alone.

His hope was that the hood would lead him straight to Johnny. Suddenly however, he noticed that the ice box door was open. It closed, revealing a thin, dark-haired young man who stepped from the refrigerator and placed two cans of beer on the table. Johnny Taylor's actual face looked exactly like the head shot Rudy had given him.

"So, how did it go? Did Uncle Rudy get everything squared away with the record people?" Johnny asked, seating himself next to the man he believed to be an ally.

"Almost," Sal grunted. "I think a couple a more days and it'll all be jake."

Johnny smiled. "Good! I'm tired of hiding out."

Sal reached into his coat. When he pulled his hand out he let loose an expletive. He looked at the empty pack of cigarettes in his huge paw with utter contempt as if the Marlboros had run off while his back was turned. "I forgot to get smokes when I was out," he bellowed. "I'll be back, kid." The bear of a man dropped his hat atop his head and left through the back door.

Rick looked about frantically. Where could he hide? There was no time. Sal would be around the corner in a second and know that he had been eavesdropping at the open window. He braced for the worst. He took a step back, assuming the fighting stance he had been taught in the army. As an MP he had been called to break up many a brawl and had become a pretty good fighter himself. But Sal was the size of a rhino. He had severe doubts that he was going to be able to take this opponent, but he steadied himself ready for the confrontation.

"Where was he?" Fifteen seconds went by and no Sal. With a sigh of relief, Rick realized that luck had been with him. The giant thug had obviously left around the other side of the bungalow. Rick wasted no time. He scurried around to the back of the house and up the three concrete steps to the kitchen door. He turned the handle. It was unlocked. Pushing open the door he burst in on the missing singer.

Johnny Taylor looked up from his can of beer obviously expecting to see Sal. "You forgot your..." he cut off mid sentence. "Who... Who are you?"

Johnny didn't know him from Adam but he pulled off the hat, glasses and fake mustache nonetheless. "My name's Rick Walker. I'm friends with your cousin Lisa. You've got to come with me. This guy isn't working with your uncle anymore. He's blackmailing him and won't tell him where you are until he pays up."

A perplexed expression crossed the singer's face but he must have had some suspicions that something was awry because after a moment he nodded and stood up. "Let me just get my things..."

"No. There's no time. We've got to go--" Rick stopped abruptly and pointed to an item on the table. "Is that Sal's wallet?"

"Yeah, he forgot it. That's why I thought you were him when you came in."

Rick hastily picked up the billfold and shoved it into the right pocket of his windbreaker. "Come on," he ordered.

Suddenly the back door flew open and the gorilla-like thug stepped inside. "I forgot my--" the eyes above the flat nose narrowed and the thin lips below it creased into a smile of recognition. "You're the kid from the hospital room." His voice was alarmingly calm. "And now you're here." He leaned against the frame of the open door. "Well at least you're familiar with the hospital 'cause I have a feelin' you're makin' a return trip real soon." Sal looked over at the table. "Where's my wallet?"

Johnny had stiffened with fear the moment Sal had returned. The realization Rick had laid upon him about the true situation had hit him like a dousing of ice water. Inadvertently, his eyes moved toward the pocket of Rick's windbreaker.

The thug knew that his wallet contained far more identifying information then he wanted in Rick's possession. "Let's have it," he growled. To punctuate his order he removed a snub nosed .38 caliber revolver from his own jacket pocket.

Johnny gasped.

Rick threw his hands up. "Alright. Alright. Take it easy." His mind raced. An idea came to him. "I'm going to slowly reach into my pocket and get your wallet. Okay?"

The goon motioned with his gun to hurry.

Keeping his right hand up Rick carefully lowered his left hand, sliding it into the pocket on the same side. There his fingers quickly and deftly loosened a drawstring. He removed his hand just as slowly but as soon as it cleared his pocket, he dumped the contents of the small pouch on the floor in front of Sal.

"What the--?" the thug uttered as dozens of marbles bounced to the floor. He took a step toward Rick but as soon as he did, the former MP moved forward grabbing the wrist holding the gun, spinning Sal further into the room as he side-stepped. The giant slid on the marbles careening wildly into the kitchen, slamming into the icebox and falling to the ground.

"Come on!" Rick yelled, grabbing Johnny by the arm and hustling him out the door. "This way!" he ordered, dragging the teen around the side of the house. By the time they were at the front of the bungalow, they heard the back door slam open. Sal was on their heels.

"Up to the boardwalk!" Rick ordered, as he and Johnny sprinted as fast as they could.

They raced the two blocks, the lumbering form of the gangster following them as quickly as he was able. When they reached the top of the ramp, Rick stopped and Vinny and Mike ran up to him.

"Hey Johnny!" Vinny said, failing to see the distress in the young man's eyes. He turned to Rick, "Well buddy, we followed you from the pizza shop and waited where you left the boards, just as you said--"

"Listen," Rick barked with authority, interrupting his friend. "He's right behind us. Mike, take Johnny down the boardwalk as fast as you can. Get off in two blocks. Get him in your car and take him to Vinny's aunt's place. Go! Hurry!" With that Johnny and Mike vanished into the thinning crowd.

Rick looked over his shoulder. Sal had almost reached the ramp. He turned back to Vinny and gave him some quick instructions. By the time the thug was halfway up the ramp, Vinny had taken off at full speed. Rick started to run but fell. It was a prat fall, meant to allow the gangster to get just a bit closer. He picked himself up and walked briskly onto Sportland Pier.

Rick threaded his way past the merry-go-round and Ferris wheel, making a beeline for one particular attraction. He approached the demonic face looming overhead, its bat-like wings spreading across the wide façade of the ride. The lighted words "Hell Hole" appeared across the very top, separated by a devilish looking pitchfork. Rick climbed the metal steps and nodded to Joey, his friend from the beach, before disappearing into the recesses of the amusement.

Sal was only a few steps behind the fleeing young man and Joey conveniently turned as he ascended the steps,

155

giving the thug the opportunity to enter without the benefit of a ticket. The moment the goon had stepped inside, Joey fastened the chain across the entranceway.

Sal entered the circular room to find that he and Rick were alone. The situation brought a broad smile to the gangster's face.

"Alright," he said. "You won. You got the kid. Now give me my wallet and we'll call it quits."

"So, I'm supposing that after I hand it over, you'll just vanish and Rudy and Johnny will never hear from you again?"

The big man scratched at his chin. "Yeah. Somethin' like that."

"Somehow I get the impression that you're the revenge type. I have my doubts that you'll simply disappear."

His huge shoulders shrugged. "I've got nothin' against the kid."

"Ah, but Rudy... that's another story, eh?"

Sal reached into his coat and produced his pistol. "I've had enough talk. Give me my wallet."

Rick waved his hand above his head and suddenly the door through which both had walked swung shut.

"What?" the gangster blurted, rushing over to the spot. He banged on the door. "Open up!" Then the circular room began to rotate. For the first time, Rick witnessed an expression of fear on the thug's face. "What gives? Stop this thing!" he yelled, pointing the gun at Rick.

The room had begun to spin faster, and Rick smiled across at his antagonist. He backed up against the padded wall.

"I'm tellin' you, get them to stop it!" he ordered Rick.

"Hey, I don't run this thing. Didn't you know what the ride was like when you came inside? That wasn't too smart, Sal."

By now the room was really whirling. The thug found himself pulled back as if by magic against the cushioned wall of the rotating room. He tried to keep the pistol fixed on Rick, but he could not withstand the laws of physics and the centrifugal force pinned his gun hand flat against the wall.

Next the bottom dropped down. The two riders spun at great speed, plastered to the padding that rimmed the amusement, suspended above the cavern that once held the floor. Rick wore a broad grin which contrasted greatly with the panicked grimace that decorated the face of the man across the diameter of the ride, the brim of his gray fedora bent upward like the hat of a slapstick comedian.

The ride spun for at least ten minutes but to the frightened gangster it seemed like an eternity. Suddenly several men in blue appeared along the observation area that sat above the rim of the spinning room. Only then did the ride begin to slow.

"We've got you covered!" one of the policeman barked. "Let go of that gun. Let it drop to the floor."

Although Sal had let go of his pistol immediately, it took a good minute for the room to slow sufficiently for the weapon to release from the wall and fall to the now restored floor. Three officers burst through the door ready to jump on the gangster but there was no fight in the big man. He slumped to the ground, gagging as if he were about to vomit.

Sportland Pier
Photos courtesy of the Wildwood Historical Society

158

Sportland Pier
Photo courtesy of the Wildwood Historical Society

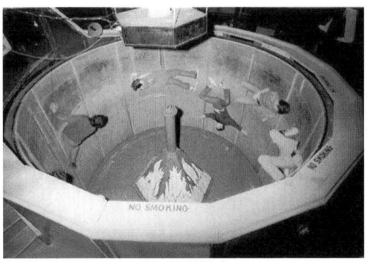

The Hell Hole
Photo courtesy of the Wildwood Historical Society

159

Chapter 12

"Too bad youse guys have to leave!" Mike said, reaching for another slice of pizza.

"Yeah, well my uncle needs his car back, and my pop could use a hand at the shop. Plus, 007 here has to get back home to Ohio."

Lisa's eyes saddened as the last sentence passed from Vinny's lips.

The gang had assembled at Sam's, Joey's favorite pizza spot. It was an ongoing argument between him and Vinny as to whether Sam's or Mack's had the best pizza on the boardwalk and despite his prejudice, even Vinny had to admit the pizza was pretty darn good. This was an opportunity for the friends to spend one last meal with Rick and Vinny, although Vinny would most certainly be back for a number of weekends as well as with his family in August.

"So," Joyce said, bubbling with excitement, "Tell us about the chase! And the arrest! I'm dying to get the scoop first hand!"

"Well," Vinny said, a hint of self importance in his voice. "Rick told me and Mike to hang back on the boardwalk while he followed this Sal character. He told us to wait at whatever street he left the boardwalk. Rick followed the guy to where he had Johnny. Johnny, tell her what happened at the house."

Johnny then stepped in and explained how Rick had come in and informed him of Sal's blackmail plot and recounted the thug's abrupt return and Rick's trick with the marbles. "Once he was down we sprinted to the boardwalk where Mike got me out of there."

"Rick told me to hustle up to Joey at the Hell Hole and if he was able to lure Sal inside, to start up the ride to trap him and then call the fuzz," Vinny continued.

"So Sal is in jail?" Joyce asked.

"Yup," Rick informed. "But I don't think he'll be inside for a very long time."

"That's why Uncle Rudy is scared stiff," Johnny added. "He's afraid that Sal will come after him as soon as he gets out. He's going to close up shop in Philly. He plans on starting anew somewhere out of the area."

"That's probably a good idea," Vinny commented. "I asked my pop if he knew this Sal character. He didn't but he asked around the neighborhood. They say he's a thug through and through and is probably less concerned about doing a little time then being disrespected by Rudy setting him up. If Rudy stayed in South Philly it's just about certain this guy would pay him a visit once he's back on the street."

"How about you, Johnny?" Rick asked. "Are you moving out with Rudy?"

"Na. I'm going to stay with Lisa's family. Her pop is a barber. He said that he'd teach me the trade."

"No more singing, then?" Mike chimed in.

Johnny shrugged. "Maybe. I don't know. But I'm not putting all of my eggs in one basket."

Joyce's brows knitted. "And that goon, Sal, is somehow responsible for Irving Shapiro's death?" she asked, before taking a sip of her lemonade.

"I don't think so. I think the old guy expired on his own; although Sal might have threatened him. I suppose it's possible that that had something to do with his heart to giving out," Rick mused. "But there would be no way of proving it."

"And Sal told Rudy that Mel took the sheet music?" Joey interjected.

"That's what he said."

Joyce shook her head. "Poor Mel. Lisa, did you hear any word about when the doctors will take him out of the induced coma?

"Actually, yes. They say he is doing well and they expect to revive him tomorrow or the next day."

"Yeah," Rick scratched his head. "That was sure weird the way he asked you about which doctor would treat him, before he passed out."

Lisa shrugged. "Sometimes people say crazy things when they're in shock."

Rick had a distant look in his eyes. He rubbed his chin as he stared off into space. Suddenly he snapped his fingers. "Lisa, take a short walk with me for a minute."

"Ah, you two. You've got the rest of the night," Vinny moaned. "Can't you wait until we're done our little party until you get some alone time?"

Rick ignored the jibe. "We'll be right back. Come on," he said, taking Lisa's hand.

"What is it?" she asked, reading the concentration on Rick's face.

"This way," he returned. "I don't want to say anything just yet, in case I'm wrong." He led her from the pizza place on 26th Street toward Juniper Avenue and then onto Hunt's Pier.

As they passed The Scrambler and The Flyer Lisa wondered what in the world Rick could be up to. He stopped in front of the Jungleland ride. Without a word, he left her side and threaded through the crowd to the very front of the attraction. There he moved past the signpost with the funny sayings and slid by one of the painted totem

162

poles. He stepped up to a figure next to a plastic palm tree; a facsimile of a native medicine man with a gaudy, painted mask upon his face. Rick looked at the figure for a moment and scratched his chin. Then he reached under the grass skirt that draped down from the seated statue's waist.

"What is he doing?" Lisa questioned aloud.

A minute later Rick was back at her side, a wide grin creasing his lips.

"What?" she asked.

He lifted his arm to reveal a folded wad of papers in his hand. "The sheet music," he declared.

Good to his word, Rick and Lisa were back at the table with their friends inside of fifteen minutes. The group was shocked, to say the least at what they had brought back with them.

"Where did you find it, again?" Joey asked in amazement, even though Rick and Lisa had already told their story.

Lisa took over. "You see, when Mel was hit by the tram car and banged his head, I told him not to worry; that he would soon be under a doctor's care. Right before he passed out, he mumbled *which doctor?* Except Rick just figured out that he wasn't asking *which doctor* would treat him; he was telling us where he hid Irving Shapiro's sheet music. It was under the *Witch Doctor* at the Jungland ride!"

"Mr. Shapiro's daughter might at least get some relief, knowing that she'll get her father's last composition back," Joyce added.

The group spent another half an hour at Sam's before moving on to the Kohr's Brothers for some frozen custard. After that they all headed up to Anglesea to the Club Avalon to take in Cozy Morley's review.

163

Cozy Morley had them laughing, despite the underlying sadness Lisa felt. She glanced over at the handsome young man as he threw his head back at one of the host's jokes. She sighed. She had had a wonderful time with him, and moreover he had rescued her cousin from what may have become a very dangerous situation.

Cozy wasn't the only comedian performing that night. Joey Bishop went on as well and his routine had them in stitches. The friends were all smiles as they exited the club that night and stepped out onto Olde New Jersey Avenue.

"Hey, I want to say something," Rick announced before the gang climbed into their cars. "It was great meeting all of you. This was the best vacation I ever had."

"Not for nothin'," Joey returned. "But you oughta dump that job at the A&P back in Ohio and just stay on here. You can get a job in like two seconds."

Rick smiled. "I wish that I could. I'm all enrolled at Ohio State for the fall. I've only got a few weeks to get everything in order. But, I think I'll explore that plan for next summer."

Lisa's eyes brightened and everyone in the crowd said they hoped that he'd be able to come back.

Rick turned toward his pal. "Hey Vin, I have to give you a special thanks. I'm really glad that you invited me." Rick said, sticking out his hand.

"No sweat! I told you you'd have a blast." Vinny reached out to shake his friend's hand but as he gripped Rick's palm it triggered a buzz that sent a shock up his arm. "Yowww!" the Italian boy yelled as he jumped a good three feet into the air.

The gang roared with laughter.

"What the--?" Vinny asked when he came back down to earth.

Rick turned up his palm to face him. "Just a souvenir from the Fun Shop on the boardwalk," he smiled.

"That's gratitude for you. I give you the best vacation of your life and that's how you repay me! Swell!" Vinny couldn't keep the grin off of his face as he gave his rebuke.

"Well now let's take a trip back in time, shall we? I seem to recall a meal when we were in West Germany, I believe we were in Bonn at the time, when someone substituted a fake rubber patty for my hamburger. Does that sound familiar?"

Vinny laughed. "Yeah. Alright. You owed me one! Come on, let's go. Get in the car, Mr. Trixter."

Fifteen minutes later the Bel Air had pulled up outside of Joyce's grandmother's house. "I know that you'll be back down here before too long," Rick said to Vinny. "But I'm sure you two still want some private time. Lisa and I are going to take a little walk down to the beach."

"Yeah. They're bugging out for *our* benefit." Vinny rolled his eyes. "Like they don't want to be alone themselves."

Rick laughed. "Either way. The girls will both be working when we leave tomorrow so this is it."

Joyce stepped out so that the couple in the back seat could exit the convertible. Appropriately, the Platters' *Goodnite Sweetheart Goodnite* could be heard drifting from the Chevy's speakers as Rick and Lisa headed up the street toward the beach.

Hand in hand they strolled. The amusement piers had closed as had the clubs. The town was much darker at this late hour allowing even more stars to wink into view.

Stepping onto the beach the alluring sound of the surf echoed toward them. As they ascended the lifeguard stand they could see the breakers softly tumbling over themselves before the white foam spread out across the hard sand in an inviting hiss. Rick took in a deep breath of salt air, saddened that it was an aroma he would only be able to revisit in his memory; at least for the foreseeable future.

The tender moments spent on the lifeguard stand that early morning were such that the couple was content to remain until the rays of the sun crept over the earth's curve. The seemingly infinite expanse of the Atlantic turned from purple to deep blue as the orb climbed, itself morphing from deep orange to bright yellow.

Later that morning Vinny and Rick bid farewell to Aunt Marie.

"Thanks for letting us stay," Rick said, giving the portly silver-haired woman a hug.

"Sure, that's okay. You earned your keep."

"I'll see you again in a few weeks when my family is down," Vinny said, as he took his turn for a hug.

The convertible backed out onto Burk Avenue and Vince gave the horn a friendly toot as he pulled away.

"So, Lisa's going to make sure that Shapiro's daughter gets that music?" Vinny asked, toying with the radio knob.

"Yup. The motel owner has her contact information."

The morning was bright and the chrome bird on the hood glistened as it pitched upward at the George Redding Bridge. As the car reached the apex Rick stole a glance back over his shoulder, making out the frame of a roller coaster and the arc of a Ferris wheel just before they disappeared as the Bel Air descended the other side of the bridge.

COZY MORLEY

Photos courtesy of the Wildwood Historical Society

Epilogue

Rick and Lisa maintained a vigorous correspondence the remainder of the summer. A weekly long-distance phone call was added that fall. Over Christmas Lisa made the trip out to Ohio for a visit. In the spring, Rick wrote with some most welcome news. Temple had accepted all of the credits from his first year at Ohio State. He would find a job in Wildwood during the upcoming summer and finish his college degree in Philadelphia.

A year after Rick graduated, they married. The couple set up house in the suburbs of Philadelphia where Rick established a successful accounting firm and Lisa worked in a doctor's office-- that is until the little ones began to arrive. Rick's business was successful enough that they purchased a summer place on Cresse Avenue.

For many decades hence summer weekends would find a circle of beach chairs on the sands of Hand Avenue where the faces were still recognizable even if the waistlines had grown and the hair had grayed. The gang of friends from South Philly passed on to their children and grandchildren what their own parents had done for them by bringing them to the Wildwoods.

Over the years some of the friends reminisced that the Wildwood of their offspring could never measure up to those golden days of the '50s and '60s when top shelf stars had made the town "Little Las Vegas." But their kids would say the same-- that the Wildwood of *their* youth outshined that of later eras. Perhaps that is why the place is so special; Wildwood impresses each generation with warm memories that are so indelible, many consider them among the best times to be had anywhere on earth.

168

If you enjoyed this story, please spread the word. Post on social media. If sales meet the threshold- more Wildwood books will follow!

Also, please patronize the George F. Boyer Museum at 3907 Pacific Avenue in Wildwood. If you are a fan of the Wildwoods you won't regret it!

Look for other books by Steve Leadley at:

www.steveleadleyauthorpage.weebly.com

Or search for him on Amazon.com

70966995R00097

Made in the USA
Columbia, SC
20 May 2017